Stepping Stones

Stepping Stones

Steve Gannon

A
KANE
BOOK

Steve Gannon

Stepping Stones

"Danny Boy" lyrics by Frederic Weatherly

Library of Congress Cataloging-in-Publication Data
Gannon, Steve.
Stepping Stones / Steve Gannon.
        p.   cm.
ISBN 978-0-9849881-5-0

Printed in the United States of America
10 9 8 7 6 5 4 3 2 1

For Susan

And in loving memory of my son
Dexter Reid Gannon

A Bag of Tools

Isn't it strange how princes and kings,
And clowns that caper in sawdust rings,
And common people like you and me,
are builders for eternity?

Each is given a list of rules;
A shapeless mass; a bag of tools
And each must fashion, ere life is flown,
A stumbling block, or a Stepping-Stone.

~ R. L Sharpe

Stepping Stones

Stories

Jessie

We stood gazing down at the bed, watching as her chest rose and fell with each click and sigh of the respirator. Neither of us knew what to say. "She's still beautiful," I ventured. It was true. The bruises under her eyes had faded, her skin had regained its glow, and despite everything that had happened you could still see the woman she had once been.

"Yes, Paul," Gordon agreed. "She is."

I heard a catch in his voice and glanced away, giving him time to compose himself.

Although Jessie and Gordon had been separated for nearly a year, neither had filed for divorce, and after the accident the burden of decision making had subsequently fallen on Gordon. I had been in Europe when it happened. Upon hearing the news, I had dropped everything and flown home to New York, then caught the first shuttle to Los Angeles. Since then I had made the trip to the West Coast three times in as many months.

I moved to the window and opened the drapes. Jessie had a private room on the fourth floor of the UCLA Medical Center that afforded a view of the city of Westwood and the glittering Pacific beyond. I watched as an onshore breeze gusted through the palms and jacarandas lining the streets below, sweeping away the brown pall that usually shrouded Los Angeles. A rarity, the sky over the City of Angels was as clear as Venetian glass, and for a dizzying instant I had the feeling I could see forever.

A moment later Dr. Robert Krasney, the neurosurgeon who had operated on Jessie, entered the room. I had met the tall, gruff man after the operation and had later spoken to him on the phone. "Paul, you know Dr. Krasney," said Gordon. "Dr. Krasney, Paul Westerfield."

"Yes, of course," said Dr. Krasney brusquely, shaking my hand. "You're Jessica's brother."

"Right." Not exactly true, but I didn't feel like getting into it.

"Dr. Krasney asked me here today to discuss Jessie's treatment," Gordon continued uneasily. "I thought we should both hear what he has to say."

"Oh?"

Dr. Krasney glanced at the bed. "There *are* things we need to discuss," he said. Seeing his face harden, I knew no false hope would come from him. He had distanced himself from our sorrow, using his medical demeanor as a mask, his professionalism as a shield.

"Has anything changed?" I asked.

Dr. Krasney hesitated. "Nothing of significance."

I have a degree in law, another in business, and in my line of work I often deal with people far more skilled in dissembling than Dr. Krasney. He was hiding something.

"Her pupillary reflex is absent, her spinal reflexes still unresponsive," the doctor went on. "As you know, she's been in a state of vegetative coma for the past three months. Because of the extensive neurologic damage she suffered, this was not unexpected."

"You told us that after the surgery," I said, wishing he would get to the point.

The police estimated that Jessie's Porsche had left the pavement on Mulholland Drive doing well over seventy. She had just finished shooting her latest movie and was driving home from a wrap party at the director's house in Malibu. She never made it back. Instead, she wound up at the bottom of a ravine with a section of doorpost buried in her skull. Since then I had learned the hard and impersonal words that described her injuries: spastic hemiplagia, brain stem dysfunction, vegetative coma.

"I think, given the circumstances, that it's time to consider moving Jessica to an institution better suited for long-term care," Dr. Krasney continued.

"Wait a minute," said Gordon. "You're saying there's no chance she'll regain consciousness?"

Dr. Krasney shook his head. "At this point, it would be extremely unlikely. And considering the neurologic damage, it's probably a blessing."

"But I've heard of cases in which comatose patients recover after *years*," Gordon persisted.

"True, but only in rare instances, and only when the neural components for consciousness are still intact. Among other things, Jessica's accident permanently damaged a structure in her brain called the ascending reticular formation, a tissue we believe to be absolutely essential for consciousness."

We had covered this ground before. "Perhaps now is not the time to bring this up," I said quietly, "but sooner or later someone has to. You're telling us Jessie has no chance of recovering, right?"

"I said it would be *extremely* unlikely."

"Is it possible for her to survive without the machines she's hooked to?"

"No."

"Then—"

"Jesus, Paul! What are you getting at?" Gordon demanded angrily.

"We all know what we're discussing," said Dr. Krasney before I could respond. He paused, gathering his thoughts. Then, glancing at me, "I sympathize, but in Jessica's case the termination of life support is not an option."

"Why?"

Gordon glared. "Damn it, Paul, you can't be suggesting—"

"I'm not suggesting anything. I just want to know why terminating life support is not even an option." I turned to Dr. Krasney, now more certain than ever that he was hiding something.

The doctor shifted uncomfortably, avoiding my eyes. "I had hoped it wouldn't be necessary to bring this up, but Jessica failed to leave a living will that would authorize withholding medical treatment in an instance such as this."

"Nevertheless," I countered, "in California it's possible to declare a patient legally dead when electrical activity ceases in

3

the brain. With the family's consent, you can then terminate life support."

"Yes. But that's the problem." Dr. Krasney finally met my gaze. "For some reason we don't fully understand, Jessica's EEG continues to show periods of electrical activity ranging from sleep-spindle clusters to states that almost resemble full consciousness. She's not aware; she can't be. But from a *legal* standpoint, because of this . . . aberration, she's still legally alive."

I felt my stomach tying in knots. "Is there a possibility she may be conscious, but just not able to—"

"No," Dr. Krasney interrupted. "I didn't mention it earlier because I didn't want to give false hope. Although we can't explain her cortical activity, we're convinced it's not significant. But unfortunately, because of it we can't pronounce her brain-dead."

"So aside from keeping her alive, there's nothing you can do?"

"That's how it stands." Dr. Krasney sighed, glancing again at the bed. "As I said, I think it's time to consider moving her to a long-term care facility." With a shrug, he started toward the door. "If you want, I can recommend several institutions in the area. Feel free to contact me when you've come to a decision."

Gordon and I made uncomfortable small talk after Dr. Krasney departed. Then Gordon left, too. I promised to call.

Afterward I stood mulling over Dr. Krasney's words. What if he was wrong about those EEG tracings? I thought. *Is it conceivable that somewhere deep inside her broken body, Jessie is still aware?*

She appeared to be asleep. Her blond hair had grown in quickly after the operation, covering most of the scars. I took her hand, feeling her fingers twitch as I did. It had happened before. Just muscular spasms, according to the doctors. Not significant. "Ah, hell, Jessie," I said aloud. "How did it ever come to this?"

I sat with her for the next hour, holding her hand and thinking back to the first time we'd met. I had been nine; she a precocious fifteen. We had only been six years apart in age. But back then, it was a lifetime.

My parents had been killed that winter in a boating accident. After the funeral I had been shipped off to live with my dad's brother Frank, who owned a small dairy in Minnesota, seventy-five miles north of Duluth. Back then the farm was way out in the sticks. I've returned recently and all that's changed, but at the time the nearest town was twenty-three miles distant and over some fairly rough road.

It was a hard time for me. I got through it, though, thanks mostly to my aunt and uncle, who took me in and treated me like their own. I remember Aunt Bev hugging me at the bus station when I arrived. She told me that she and Uncle Frank loved me, and that although she knew they could never replace my parents, she hoped someday I would come to think of them as my new mom and dad. And in time, I did.

Jessica, their only daughter, proved a different story. Cousin or not, she made it clear right off the bat that she was *not* my sister, and she didn't want a nine-year-old kid hanging around her. Maybe she was jealous of the attention given to me by her parents; maybe it was simply our difference in age. I never knew.

Of course, I immediately fell in love with her.

Despite Jessie's being the worst tomboy in the county, it was obvious to everyone that she was going to be a heartbreaker. But there was something else about her, something special. I think what drew me most, for lack of a better word, was her spirit. Even back then she had a quality about her that set her apart. Later in her life it came across on the silver screen, alive and true, something you could hold in your mind long after the lights in the theater came on. It won her an Academy Award; it made her a star.

Anyway, I spent that first long winter tagging after my precocious cousin, usually fifty yards or so behind. All that changed one cold, dismal day the following spring.

We had a three-mile walk down a dirt road to a crossroads where the bus picked us up for school. In winter we could shave that distance by taking a path through the pines and crossing the frozen river. We were forbidden to go that way, so naturally we always did, provided the snow hadn't drifted too deep. That day after school we had ridden the bus back to the crossroads. From there Jessie had headed into the woods on foot, taking the shortcut. By then the ice covering the river had thinned in spots, and I worried every time we crossed it. Nonetheless, I trudged along behind, keeping my customary distance. I figured Jessie knew what she was doing. After all, she *was* fifteen.

The sun was slipping behind the mountains when we reached the river, and a chilling wind had picked up. Eager to get home, I increased my pace. All of a sudden I noticed a man in the woods following Jessie, paralleling her course along the riverbank. He looked like one of the pulp-mill workers who had drifted into town earlier that winter, hoping for work. He hadn't seen me. I fell back, wondering what he was doing.

He stayed concealed in the trees, taking care to remain hidden until Jessie broke into a clearing by the river. I should have done something—called out, warned her, run for help—but I didn't. I was too frightened.

And then it was too late.

He caught up with her in an instant. I froze, unable to move. Jessie struggled, fought like a cat. I heard him laugh as he doubled his fist and hit her. Then he jerked her jacket over her head, covering her face and trapping her arms. Brutally, he yanked her jeans down around her ankles and ripped off her underwear. Jessie was crying but she kept fighting, kicking blindly with her feet. The man held her down and punched into her jacket until she lay still. Then he undid his belt.

It was over in minutes. Although I couldn't move, I couldn't tear my eyes from the horror, either. I just . . . watched. As long as I live, I will never forget my feelings that day of helplessness, self-loathing, and despair.

When he finished, the man pulled up his pants and fastened his belt. Jessie lay at his feet, her legs smeared with blood. He lifted her, hefting her over his shoulder. Then he set out on the frozen river toward a hole fishermen had cut the previous weekend. We had passed it every day on the way to school, and I knew only a thin film of ice now covered it. With a sinking feeling, I realized that the man didn't intend to let Jessie go.

I had to do something. *But what?* I was no match for him, and if I revealed myself he would kill me as well. Nonetheless, I couldn't simply stand by as he took her life. Without thinking, I grabbed a baseball-sized chunk of river rock and slipped out onto the ice behind him.

I had a good arm for a kid. I hoped if I could get close enough, I could stun him enough to give us time to get away. Not much of a plan, but it was all I could come up with. The trouble was, he had Jessie slung over his shoulder, blocking a clear shot at his head. Jessie had worked one arm free and was struggling again, making things even worse. At one point she turned toward me, and for a terrible instant I saw the terror in her eyes. She knew where he was taking her, too.

Only a few yards remained to the hole. I crept forward, my heart pounding. When I got in range I eased out to the side for a better shot. Knowing I would only have one chance, I held my breath, wound up, and threw as hard as I could—stepping into it, putting all my weight behind that throw.

The man must have seen a flicker of movement just as I released the rock. At the last moment, he twisted.

The stone glanced off his temple. It hurt him, but not enough.

I stood dumbfounded. He whirled to face me. "You little bastard," he snarled, wiping blood from his forehead. Then he grinned. I knew we'd both just had the same realization: *I was out of rocks, and I couldn't outrun him.*

He covered the last yards to the hole in a heartbeat. Jessie screamed as he threw her in. With a cracking sound, her body broke through the ice. Then he turned to me. I shot a look at the shoreline, knowing I would never make it. Even if I did, he would catch me in the woods. I hesitated, then turned and sprinted for the center of the river, heading for the thin section of ice we had been avoiding all week. I hoped he would follow.

He did.

He had almost caught me when the ice abruptly gave way beneath him. Narrowly avoiding going in myself, I stood on the creaking surface, watching him thrash in the freezing water.

Then I remembered Jessie.

Praying she was still alive, I made a wide circle around the broken area and returned to the hole where he had thrown her in. I found her clinging to the side. The river was flowing sluggishly beneath the ice, but with enough force to drag her legs under the edge. "Jessie, hang on!" I yelled, scrabbling through a pile of firewood the fishermen had left. I needed a piece long enough the span the hole. The best I found was a four-foot length of two-by-four.

Too short. Maybe onshore.

"Hang on!" I yelled again, starting for the woods. "I'll be back in a minute."

"No time," Jessie mumbled, her teeth chattering. "Can't hold on. Get me out now."

The current was pulling her under.

Stretching out on the ice, I extended my hand. She took it. Her grip felt weak, her skin cold as death. "My wrist, Jessie," I shouted. "Grab my wrist!"

"Wha . . . ?"

"The fireman's grip. I can't hold you otherwise."

Shifting her hand, she grasped my wrist, and I hers. It felt solid, but I knew I didn't have the strength to pull her out. "You have to help."

"I can't."

"Throw a leg over the edge. You can do it."

"I can't."

"Yes, you can," I said, willing it to be true. "You have to. Do it, Jessie. Now."

Slowly, painfully, using my hand for leverage, Jessie struggled from the hole. Finally she rolled onto the ice. Shivering violently, she pulled on her wet clothes, covering her nakedness. I gave her my jacket. Then, without warning, a crack sounded on the ice behind us, followed by the sound of something else. Something moving.

Jessie wasn't the only one who had made it out.

Somehow the man had managed to pull himself up onto the ice. Moving on his hands and knees, he started toward us.

After all that, I thought bitterly, *we're no better off than before.*

All at once the surface gave way beneath him again.

With a surge of relief, I headed for the shore. Jessie didn't follow.

Puzzled, I turned back. "Jessie, let's go!"

"No."

Fighting panic, I returned and began tugging her arm. "Please," I begged. "Let's go!"

"No, Paul. He'll get out again. He'll catch us before we reach the road."

I knew she was right. The best we could do was split up. Maybe one of us would escape. "What do you want to do?" I asked, my voice trembling.

She picked up the two-by-four I had discarded. "Stop him."

I followed her out on the ice. Jessie was right. By the time we reached him, the man had moved to a thicker section and already had a leg up over the edge. I watched as Jessie raised the two-by four and brought it crashing down.

She drove him back into the water. Blood poured from his nose, staining the river around him. But he was strong. He wouldn't give up.

But every time he came close to making it out, Jessie was there.

He lasted about fifteen minutes, maybe a little more. I saw the fury bleed from his eyes, turning to surprise, then pleading, and finally to despair as he realized he was going to die. In the end the current simply took him under the ice. We watched as his shadow drifted downriver beneath the surface.

"Jesus," I said, trying hard not to cry.

Jessie threw her bloody club into the water. It bobbed a second; then the current took it away, too. After it disappeared, she put her arms around me and held me tightly. I could feel her body shaking under her wet clothes.

"You saved my life," she said quietly.

I looked away, feeling a hot rush of shame. "I . . . I wanted to do something earlier, but I . . ."

"You saved my life," she repeated firmly. "I'll never forget it. Never." Then her voice hardened. "I had to do what I did. He would have caught us and . . . I couldn't let him get out. You understand, don't you?"

I nodded, not trusting myself to speak.

"Then it's over. We're not going to tell anyone about this."

"But you're hurt. What will you say to your folks?"

"I'll make something up. Please, Paul. I don't think anyone would understand, not really. And even if they did . . . Listen, I just want to put this behind us. Please. Will you promise not to tell?"

I thought for a long, searching moment.

"Say it, Paul."

I hesitated a moment more. Finally I took a deep breath and nodded. "I promise," I said.

Neither of us ever spoke again of that day, but it wasn't forgotten. I kept my promise, and it became a covenant of trust between us, a bond that drew us together, something we shared alone. And through all the years that followed, after Dad died and Mom sold the farm to one of the big conglomerates that took over in the late sixties, after Jessie moved to California and I to New York, it held us still.

I spent most of the evening sitting in the hospital room holding Jessie's hand, remembering. I did a lot of talking, too. It didn't matter that she couldn't hear; it just felt good being with her. As I rambled, I gradually became aware that her fingers were twitching again—not all of them, just her index and middle fingers. First one, then the other.

One, two.

One, two.

Let your fingers do the walking.

"Jessie, can you hear me?"

One, two.

10

I sat up, suddenly alert.

One, two.

All at once I understood. I released her hand and allowed her fingers to inch up my arm. Seconds later her hand opened slightly, then closed on my wrist. With a shock of recognition, I closed my hand too, completing the fireman's grip.

"Oh, God," I whispered. I tried to swallow but couldn't. Her face hadn't changed, but her grip was stronger now, unmistakable. Perhaps she simply sensed my presence, perhaps she only recognized the sound of my voice, but of one thing I was certain: Jessie knew I was there. And with a feeling of horror, I realized something else.

Jessie wasn't just telling me that she was aware. She was asking something of me as well.

Once again, she was asking me to save her.

"I can't, Jess," I said softly, wondering why no one had noticed this before. Was it only sometimes that Jessie rose to consciousness, or . . .

Her grip tightened.

I sat for several minutes, trying to sort things out. If this were something new, did it really change anything? Jessie was still unable to move, to see, to breathe on her own—forever entombed in a body that for all intents and purposes was a prison. I tried to imagine the suffocating horror she must be experiencing . . . and failed.

Finally I put my lips to Jessie's ear and told her that I loved her. I told her that I needed time to think. I told her that I was afraid. But only after I promised to come back, *no matter what I decided*, did she relax her grip.

I spent the remainder of the evening in the hospital cafeteria drinking coffee and watching bleary-eyed medical personnel drifting in and out on their breaks. Repeatedly, I ran it over in my mind. Jessie was aware, at least part of the time, but imprisoned in her own body . . . without light, without hope.

How long had she lain there, struggling to cry out?

And now she wanted me to end it.

11

I knew from her grip what she was asking of me. I knew it as surely as if she had spoken aloud. Again, I felt like a frightened boy cringing in the woods, wanting to help but too terrified to move. Yet I knew I couldn't abandon her now, any more than I could then. But could I bring myself to do what she wanted?

And even if I could . . . did I have that right? Did anyone?

The horizon was awash with the first glimmers of dawn as I rode the elevator back up to the ICU unit. Numbly, I walked down the corridor, nodding to the bright young faces at the nurses' station as I passed. After all these months they knew me by name, didn't care that I was there before visiting hours.

Moments later I stood outside Jessie's room. Across the hallway, the door to another room stood open, the bed beyond deserted. Gazing out a window beside the bed, I watched as the sun began to rise on a new day, absently thinking that it's a blessing men don't have the power to gaze into the future. I hesitated for what seemed an eternity, searching my conscience.

Then, at last, I opened Jessie's door and stepped inside.

The Green Monkey

The evening sun had settled low on the horizon when I noticed Christy Sullivan and her mother pulling their handcart up the dirt road. Curious, I watched from the solitude of the Farraguts' barn as they approached. I could see that fourteen-year-old Christy was doing most of the pulling, head lowered, a determined set to her shoulders. She had on a blue hand-me-down dress that had been patched many times and looked too big on her. When they got closer, I could also see from the dusty smears on her cheeks that she had been crying.

I was working on Sandy Farragut's mare at the time. She'd gone lame a few days back. The big bay was part of a matched pair Sandy was mighty proud of, and he wanted her back in front of his buggy as soon as possible. I'd done my share of work for Sandy over the past year, and as he was both my patron and one of my biggest clients, I aimed to oblige.

Eighteen months earlier I had started taking care of the Farraguts' livestock for my room and board. Before long word had spread that I was good with animals, and now I'm doing vet work for most of the town. In a farming community like Danville, animals are near as important as people—sometimes even more so—and I've done well. In a few years I may have enough saved for a small place of my own. I've done well, all right, but I've kept to myself. I have no friends in Danville, not really. I prefer it that way.

I was making progress with Sandy's mare, but curiosity finally got the better of me and I stepped from the barn and out into the yard. By then Christy and her mother had their cart pulled over in the shade by the main house. Mrs. Sullivan spotted me as I rounded the corner.

"Howdy, Seth," she said.

"Evenin', Mrs. Sullivan." Mary Sullivan was a tall, attractive woman in her late thirties, but farm life had left her looking older than her years. Her face was filled with concern, but I could tell from the way she kept glancing at her daughter that it was Christy she was worried about, not the injured dog in the cart.

Without being asked, I examined the dog. A farm breed, he appeared to be mostly Irish Setter with something else thrown in, maybe Australian Shepherd or Border Collie. He was a handsome animal—shiny tan and white fur, brown eyes, intelligent face. Blood had seeped from his mouth to form a dark puddle beside his head. One of his legs was flopped off at an angle, and I could see bone sticking through the fur. His gums were white and he was panting, rapid and shallow, like he couldn't get his breath. I didn't need to search around inside to tell he was dying.

"Can you fix him, Mr. Neuman?" Christy asked, her eyes holding mine, willing me to say yes.

I looked away. I knew from her expression that her dog was probably the most important thing in her life, at least right then, and I didn't know what to say.

"Can you?"

Turning back, I regarded her again, struck by something in her deep blue eyes that reminded me of Ma. "What's his name?" I asked.

"Lucky."

"Lucky, huh?" I said, skipping the obvious comment. "Well, he's hurt bad, Christy. You know that."

She swallowed hard, fighting tears. "Yes, sir."

Mrs. Sullivan placed her hand on my arm. "Seth, may I speak with you in private?"

"Sure, Mrs. Sullivan."

Christy's eyes followed us as we walked to the corral. When we were out of earshot of her daughter, Mrs. Sullivan said, "I don't know how to tell you this, Seth." She stood for a moment worrying a loose thread on her sweater. "We . . . we've been having a hard time of it this past year, what with crop prices and that dry spell and all. Fact is we just don't have any money to pay for doctoring that dog. He means a whole lot to the girl, but we just . . ." Her voice trailed off. Then she shrugged sadly. "I reckon he's dyin' anyway. I would appreciate it if you'd just put him down."

I looked across the yard. Christy was leaning over the cart ministering to Lucky, her hands trying to give comfort. I watched briefly, then came to a decision. "There won't be any charge for the doctoring," I said.

"You don't have to do that, Seth."

"I know, Mrs. Sullivan. I want to."

She gazed at me for a long moment, then smiled sadly. "Well, thank you, Seth. And God bless you."

I turned away. *God has already blessed me*, I thought bitterly. *Blessed me and damned me in the same stroke.* "Tell me what happened," I said.

"It was an accident," Mrs. Sullivan answered, seeming to sense by my change of mood. When I remained silent, she shook her head and went on. "Christy and Lucky were down by the landing watching workers unload the barges. I reckon you heard what happened up at Auger's Crossing. People have been heading downriver steady for the past couple days now. Anyhow, Lucky was chasing some livestock and got caught under one of the big wagon wheels. Wasn't nobody's fault."

A chill ran through me. It was a cool evening, but I could feel sweat beading on my forehead. "What happened at Auger's Crossing?"

"You didn't hear?"

"No."

"Well, it looks like the radiation poison is showing up again. Imagine, after all these years. Nobody can figure where it's coming from, but all of a sudden lots of folks there are coming down with cancer. Them that's able are leaving as fast as they can."

"What kind of cancer?" I asked, trying to keep my voice steady.

"Bone, I think," she answered, eyeing me curiously. "Fifteen so far. Come to think of it, you're from up that way, aren't you? Got any kin there?"

I nodded.

15

"Sorry to hear that."

"Yeah," I said. "Me, too."

I walked back to the cart. Mrs. Sullivan followed. On the way over I thought about what she'd said. I had tried to forget what had happened upriver, but I guess some things won't stay forgotten. In the back of my mind I'd always known it was sure to surface. Now it had.

Fifteen men.

That left four still to go.

Christy glanced up when I returned. I didn't make her ask. "I'm going to do my best to help Lucky," I said. A hollow feeling welled up inside me as I watched her eyes fill with the tears she had held back earlier.

Christy and Mrs. Sullivan helped me get the dog into the barn. We laid him on a clean bed of straw and covered him with a horse blanket. Then I waited till they were gone. Next, before starting, I steadied myself for what was to come. I needed to find out how bad the dog was hurt, and there was only one way to do it. Taking a deep breath, I sent my mind into him, steeling myself against his pain as my senses seeped into his suffering.

Fighting the impulse to withdraw, I closed my eyes and began my search. His heart was racing in quick, hurried strokes, not doing much good. Blood was pooling in his abdomen, and not enough was returning to his heart for it to beat properly. There were two main areas of bleeding—one in a kidney, another in an artery running to the broken leg.

I repaired them as quickly as I could.

Next I decreased the blood flow to several other injured organs and constricted some of the surface vessels, too—getting the pressure up enough so his heart could work right. At that point I began to think Christy's dog had a chance. But as I continued to explore his injuries, I discovered I couldn't feel anything in his hind legs. I couldn't make them move, either. Working my way back up the big nerve bundle in his spine, I found the problem. Several vertebra had been shattered by the wagon wheel, crushing the nerves inside.

Lucky's other injuries could wait. If he were ever to walk again, I had to mend the spinal nerves right away. "Take it easy, pup," I said. I smoothed the fur on his head and took away the pain. I had found out what I needed to know; there wasn't any reason he shouldn't be comfortable. I still felt his suffering, though, as sharp and penetrating as ever. I had never learned to get around that.

"Go to sleep, boy," I whispered, giving him another nudge with my mind. He let out a long sigh and closed his eyes.

By then the sun had set, but I didn't bother lighting the lantern. For what I had to do, I didn't need to see. Night gradually enveloped us. I remained on the straw beside Christy's dog, linked together with him as if we were one. And gradually, as I worked, the pain I felt flowing from him began to ease. And as it did, I allowed my thoughts to drift back to Auger's Crossing, back to the day that had forever changed my life.

*   *   *

Come hell or high water, Pa had decided we were going to move that boulder in the north field.

It was one of his projects, one of the ones he would dream up whenever he had a skinful of liquor—like the time he decided we were going to dam the river. It couldn't be done, but it was easier to just go along than try to persuade Pa otherwise. Right from the start I knew this was going to be another of his fiascos. We had been plowing around that rock for as long as I could remember, just like Grandpa had, and Grandpa's father before him. It was just too big to move.

We had cut our hay weeks earlier, but then the rains had come with a vengeance, preventing us from getting our crop off the ground. Eventually the sun had come out, once more turning the weather hot and dry, and we'd finished the harvest at last. As far as I was concerned the season was over, but Pa unexpectedly announced that we had one more chore. We were going to move that rock before the ground froze, and there was no use arguing.

17

Georgie woke me at first light. "Seth, get up," he whispered, lowering his voice so's not to disturb Pa. He needn't have bothered. Pa had spent most of the previous night at the tavern. Since Ma had died he'd taken to drinking there on a regular basis, and it was a safe bet he wouldn't be up before noon.

"Lemme sleep, Georgie," I mumbled. "We don't have to start this early."

"C'mon, Seth. Let's surprise Pa. Let's do it all by ourselves."

Aw, Georgie . . ."

"Please, Seth."

I propped myself up on one elbow, squinting in the half-light at my older brother Georgie. He was big, with thick blond hair that stuck up in back in the worst cowlick you ever saw. He had a huge grin on his face, and I could tell he was excited. Georgie saw moving that rock as a chance to please Pa. He didn't understand it was just too big to move. Georgie didn't understand a lot of things.

I had turned fifteen earlier that summer. Georgie was four years older than me and half again my weight, but I still thought of him as my little brother. "Okay," I groaned, realizing there was no way I would be getting any more sleep that morning. "I'm getting up."

We dressed quickly, pulling on our clothes over the long johns we had worn to bed. It took me longer to get ready than Georgie because I had to take a couple new turns of tape around my boots. I needed a new pair, but there never seemed to be enough money. Although tape was cheaper than boots, things from the city, even tape, were getting harder to come by.

We left the cabin out the back door, Georgie making sure the screen didn't bang. With the sun barely peeking over the ridge, we crossed the old wagon road and headed up our shortcut along the creek to the north field. It was a crisp fall morning, so clear and cold it stung my nose when I breathed it in. A mist hung over the stream, drifting in and out of the oaks on either side. The crows were already up and scolding us from high in the trees, their metallic cries echoing in the still mountain air.

Minutes later a breeze began moving up from the valley below. Georgie was ahead of me on the trail, a pick in one hand and a heavy oak beam slung over his shoulder with the other. Although I was only carrying a pair of shovels, I was having trouble keeping up. "Georgie, slow down," I called.

"C'mon, Seth, we're almost there," he hollered back, his words filled with excitement. I sighed and tried to keep him in sight.

We finally emerged from the woods, stepping into the field we shared with Abe McClintock and his two sons. Over the years, plowed-up stones had been piled in the center, forming a rock wall that divided the acreage. The two parcels were roughly equal, with one exception: A gigantic boulder sat right in the middle of ours. The McClintock clan had been ribbing us Neumans about it for generations. Pa aimed to change that.

Georgie and I walked to the rock. As I said, we had been plowing around it for years, but now that we were going to try digging it up, I decided to take a better look. Most rock in the valley was shale and sandstone. The boulder before me was solid granite, with large black crystals peppered throughout. One side was flattened and appeared to have been smoothed somehow, with shallow, parallel grooves cut into its polished surface. It stood about my height and was even broader at the base. Maybe Pa thought we could roll it or something, but I knew different. It wasn't going anywhere.

Nonetheless, we dug.

Georgie swung the pick and I shoveled, following him around the boulder and digging out the stones and dirt that he loosened. The soil was still damp from the rains and had a rich, dark smell. Every once in a while I could see sparks fly from the pick when Georgie hit a stone. We worked steadily, cutting through the alfalfa stubble and topsoil. Deeper down it got rocky and our progress slowed.

By eleven, with the sun now high in the sky, we were three feet down all around the boulder. It hadn't constricted at the base as I'd hoped. If anything, it had grown broader.

"We're gettin' there, huh, Seth?" Georgie asked.

"We're getting there," I answered, feeling a renewed surge of anger at Pa for involving us in another of his hopeless schemes. Leaning on my shovel, I checked our progress. There wasn't much. By then I had worked up a good sweat, so I stripped off my shirt and long john top. Georgie kept working.

I sat on the edge of the trench, watching Georgie swing the pick. He moved with an easy rhythm, his arms and back rolling with a smooth, animal-like grace. He had a relaxed grin on his face and was clearly enjoying himself. Georgie was like that. He would get on a job and stick with it till it was done, smiling the whole time.

"Take a break, Georgie."

He shook his head, never missing a stroke. "No, Seth. I want to get done before Pa gets here."

"Georgie, we're never gonna move this rock."

He stopped swinging, a confused frown replacing his smile. "But Pa said we were."

"Right," I backtracked, deciding not to get into it. Grabbing my shovel, I dropped back into the trench. "Let's get to work."

We dug. The sun got hotter, the trench got deeper, and the rock got bigger. Pa showed up around noon, a jar of corn liquor in one hand. With stubborn, narrowed eyes, he surveyed the boulder. I could tell from his scowl that it was larger than he'd figured.

"We tried to dig it up before you got here," Georgie said from waist-deep in the trench.

Pa stared at the boulder. "Damn," he said, taking a pull on his jar.

"Bigger'n you reckoned, huh?" I said.

Pa took another pull on his jar.

"Face it, Pa," I went on. "It ain't gonna happen."

Pa spit on the ground, and I saw that look come over his face. I had seen it plenty of times before.

"We'll get the goddamned thing moved if it's the last thing we do," he said.

"Right, Pa," said Georgie, nodding in agreement. "We'll get 'er moved."

"Shut up," Pa snapped. "Gimme that pick." Shoving Georgie out of the way, he dropped into the trench, acting as if he were the only one in creation who knew how to dig. Scowling, he attacked the rocky soil. At the rate he started off, I figured he'd be good for less than an hour.

"I'm sorry we didn't get it done before you got here, Pa," said Georgie. "We tried real hard."

Pa stopped swinging. He glared at Georgie, then resumed digging. I climbed into the trench behind him and shoveled, wondering how things had ever grown so bad between us.

Actually, I knew, but I didn't want to think about it. It had started when Ma died. She had been the glue that held our family together. After she'd gone, things just fell apart. Not that things had been great before that—not by a long shot. I used to hear Ma and Pa fighting late at night, long after Georgie and I were supposed to be asleep.

Mostly they fought about Georgie.

"It ain't right, a boy being able to do what he does," I heard Pa say one night. "If anybody was to find out, it wouldn't go easy on us. They'd probably burn us out. Maybe worse."

"What do you want to do, John?" Ma asked softly. "Turn him in?"

"No, nothin' like that," Pa answered quickly. "But for the life of me, I don't understand why God saw fit to burden us with an abomination."

Ma wasn't partial to the beliefs some folks held—especially if those beliefs led to somebody getting hurt—and that kind of talk got her riled. Ma and Pa went at it in earnest after that.

I was eight at the time, but old enough to know they weren't fighting about Georgie's being slow. It was because he could make things move.

Ma said it wasn't God or Satan that caused it. It was the poison. After the war it seeped into the ground and got carried by the water till it was just about everywhere—not just the big cities, but everywhere—and odd things began to happen. I've seen pictures in Grandpa's books of two-headed babies and the like. Some of the livestock births were even stranger, and there were other things as well. You'd hear rumors every once in a while about happenings that most of our neighbors considered against God and nature. Things like what Georgie could do.

One day Pa caught Georgie and me playing a game down by the creek. We were winging mud clods at an empty whiskey jug on the opposite bank. Georgie had it floating unsupported a couple feet over the ground. He was making it jump back and forth so no matter where we threw, we almost always scored a hit. We were laughing so hard we didn't hear Pa approaching.

Pa came out of the woods and saw what we were doing. He put the belt to both of us, then dragged us crying back to Ma.

After sending Pa away, Ma sat us down on the hearth. Sitting didn't feel especially good after the licking Pa had just given us, but we sat anyway. I was mad. Georgie was crying. He didn't understand what we had done wrong.

Ma put her arm around him. I remember she didn't seem angry, just concerned. It was as though she had been expecting it. "I'm going to tell you boys a story," she said, speaking softly like she always did when she had something important to say. We leaned closer to hear.

"Georgie, do you know what a monkey is?" she asked.

"You mean like the picture in Grandpa's book?" Georgie sniffed, wiping his nose on his sleeve.

"Right. A monkey's an animal that lived a long time ago, long before the Change."

"Are there any left?" I asked, glad the conversation seemed to have veered from our game on the bank.

"I don't know, honey," Ma answered. "Maybe somewhere. Anyway, monkeys used to live together in groups. Each group was big, like our family and all our neighbors put together. Understand, Georgie?"

"Uh-huh."

"Good. Now, all the monkeys in the group knew one other, and they all got along fine, like a big family. Then one day some men caught one of the younger monkeys in a trap. They poked and teased him. When they tired of that, they decided to play a trick. They mixed up a big bucket of green dye and dumped it on him. They left him in the trap all day. When the monkey was finally dry, his fur had turned bright green. Then the men let him go, laughing at him as he ran back into the forest to rejoin his group.

"Can you guess what happened next, Georgie? No? Well, the other monkeys wouldn't let him come back. Even his own brothers and sisters wouldn't accept him. They drove him out."

By then Georgie had stopped crying. "Why, Mama?" he asked. "Didn't they know him?"

"Oh, they knew him," Ma said slowly. "It was just that now he looked different. He was different from them, and they didn't want him anymore."

"But why?"

"Because they were afraid, I guess. He was different from them, and they were afraid. That's just the way things are. People around here are that way, too."

"I don't like this story, Mama."

"You don't have to like it, honey, as long as you learn something from it. Besides, the story's not done yet."

Ma was mostly speaking to Georgie, but every now and then she would gaze over at me. I'll never forget her eyes. They were deep, deep blue shot through with tiny flecks of gold. Sometimes, like then, I felt they could see right through me and straight into my heart. Suddenly I realized her story was also meant for me. She knew Georgie wasn't the only one who was different. Even back then, even before I learned what I could do, she knew.

"So the young monkey was all alone," Ma continued. "He lived outside the group and was very, very unhappy. Then one day the rains came. It rained all day and all night. It rained so hard that it washed every bit of green from the monkey's fur. The next morning he looked normal. His fur was a nice brown color once more. When he returned to his group they were happy to see him and let him come back."

Georgie sat quietly, thinking about Ma's story.

"Georgie?"

"Yes, Mama?"

"Do you understand what I'm trying to tell you?"

"I'm not sure."

"Georgie, nobody else can make things move like you can," she said. "You're the only one. You're the one who's different."

All at once Georgie understood. He started crying again. "I don't want to be the green monkey," he sobbed.

"Shhh, honey. You don't have to. Nobody can tell just from looking at you, and we're going to keep it a secret, okay? You'll never do it anymore, and we won't let anyone know, all right? Will you promise?"

Georgie nodded, tears spilling down his cheeks. "I promise, Mama."

Georgie never made anything move again, but sometimes when we were off by ourselves and nobody could see, we played other games. Georgie learned he could wrap himself up in that power of his, wearing it like an invisible skin. When he had it on, it made him as slippery as creek-bottom mud. Nothing could touch him. He could go swimming in his clothes without getting wet, pick up a hot coal and not get burned, things like that.

We were careful, and we never again got caught. But it was easier for me than Georgie. The things I was learning to do didn't show . . . not on the outside, anyway.

Ma took sick three years later. She died not long after that. Toward the end I used to sit with her in the morning before my chores, and again in the evening before going to bed. As I held her hand, I could feel the cancer spreading through her. I tried to understand how it could be a part of her and yet still destroy her. I wanted to understand, hoping I could stop it. I tried. I didn't know how but I tried, and I kept trying until the pain grew too great and I couldn't stand it anymore.

Ma knew what I was doing. I never told her, but like everything else, she knew.

After Ma died Pa took to drinking. Georgie and I handled the farm chores, and I watched out for Georgie. Pa and I got further apart. We lived together but we weren't a family . . . not after Ma died.

I was wrong about Pa. He only lasted twenty minutes before climbing out of the trench and reaching for his jar. By then he was dripping sweat and the skin on the back of his neck had turned an angry pink from the sun.

Georgie and I had been taking turns shoveling while Pa swung the pick. As soon as Pa quit, Georgie grabbed the pick. I kept shoveling. Pa retired to the shade with his jar and quickly reduced its contents by half.

While Pa rested, we kept at it. Some fair-sized rocks slowed our progress and we used the beam that Georgie had brought to lever them out. By late afternoon we were down five feet all the way around, and the base of the rock was finally beginning to cut back in. Ten feet of solid granite lay uncovered. From the looks of it, four more still remained in the dirt.

"What the hell you dog turds doin'?"

Squinting up, I saw Jake McClintock, the younger of the McClintock boys, gawking over the edge of the trench. He had his back to the sun, blocking it with his huge bulk. He leaned over the trench a bit more, knocking dirt on Georgie. "Sorry about that, swifty," he laughed, his tone saying otherwise.

"What's it look like we're doing, Jake?" I asked. "And his name isn't swifty." Jake and his brother were always teasing Georgie about being slow. I didn't like Jake much. Fact is, I didn't like any of the McClintocks.

"Oh, *excuse* me," said Jake with a nasty grin. "And since you ask, it looks to me like you two retards are tryin' to dig up that boulder.

Pa wove his way up behind Jake. "Mind your own business," he ordered. In the backlight I could see spittle spraying from Pa's lips. I smiled as I saw some of it land on Jake.

"My old man already thinks you Neumans are loco," Jake hooted, ignoring Pa's warning. "Wait'll he hears about this!"

"Get off my land," Pa hissed, stumbling as he bent for a stone to send Jake packing.

Jake turned and sauntered off, keeping an eye on Pa's throwing arm as he left, his laughter mocking us as he disappeared into the woods.

"Snot-nosed McClintock whelp," Pa called after him, his face flushed with anger.

By then the sun was low in the sky, and cool gusts from the high plateau were spilling down the valley. I sighed, realizing from Pa's flinty scowl that we would probably be there all night.

"Bring that beam over here," Pa commanded, dropping into the trench. "Time to get this sonofabitch out."

Although Georgie and I'd had a tough time levering out some of the smaller rocks we'd encountered, we went ahead and did what Pa ordered, clearing away the loose diggings and getting the beam positioned as best we could. Despite our efforts, anybody could see it was set up wrong. We couldn't get a fulcrum low enough, and the beam was too short to be a proper lever. It was like trying to move a house with a broom handle. Nonetheless, we tried. It was easier than arguing with Pa.

At one point, while Pa and I wrestled with the beam, Georgie went around to cut more dirt from the backside of the boulder. Unexpectedly, the boulder shifted. Georgie had undermined the rock enough to let it lurch forward, right on top of him.

"Georgie!" I screamed. Pa and I rushed to the other side. Georgie was trapped under the boulder. But it wasn't *on* him. A space showed between him and the stone.

Suddenly I realized what had happened. At the last instant Georgie must have put on his "skin," and it had saved him. "Hang on, Georgie," I yelled. "We'll get you out."

"I'm okay, Seth. I think I can move it."

"What?"

"I can move it," he repeated. "Watch me, Seth."

Speechless, Pa and I watched as Georgie shoved the boulder to the other side of the pit. But he didn't shove it. It just . . . *moved.*

Georgie climbed from the hole. "I did it," he said, grinning like a kid. "Did you see me?"

"We saw you," I said, staring in amazement.

Pa remained silent, lost in thought. Then he asked, "Can you move it out of the pit?"

Georgie frowned. "I don't know, Pa. I promised Mama I wouldn't make anything move. I shouldn't have done it."

"The boulder was on top of you," I pointed out. "You had to."

"Yeah, but—"

"Listen, Georgie," Pa interrupted. "I'm your father, and I'm telling you it's all right. You've already done it once. Do it again. Ma wouldn't mind."

Georgie glanced at me. I shrugged, thinking he couldn't do it anyway. Shifting the boulder was one thing; lifting it was another.

"Okay," said Georgie. His eyes went vacant, as if he were thinking about something that had happened a long time back. A split second later Pa and I scrambled out of the way as the boulder came floating hole!

Looking like a huge, prehistoric tooth that had somehow been ripped from the earth, it hovered three feet above the pit, the bottom third covered with dirt, my shirt and long johns still on top where I'd thrown them. Pa danced around the stone, gleefully slapping his thigh. "Over there, Georgie," he shouted, pointing to the rock wall dividing our field from the McClintocks' acreage. "Over there!"

Grinning, Georgie trailed along behind the boulder, dwarfed by the giant rock as it floated toward the center of the field.

"Set it on top," Pa ordered. "Right on top, Georgie. Right on top!"

Recalling Ma's story, I stood numbly, a premonition of disaster gnawing at my insides as Georgie set the boulder atop the boundary wall. It settled onto the loose stones, thrusting them aside as it descended, shattering the larger rocks below and sending stone fragments flying in all directions. The smell of powdered rock filled my nose as the boulder continued to settle, coming to rest when it had reburied itself a couple of feet in the soft earth.

"By God, we did it!" Pa roared, thumping Georgie on the back. "We did it! Boys, we're celebrating tonight. Tonight you're going to the tavern with me."

Georgie was beaming with pride. I'd never seen him happier. "Pa, there's a problem," I said, not wanting to ruin the moment but knowing I had to speak. "People will ask how we did it. What are you gonna tell them?"

"Hell," Pa snorted, "I'll tell 'em we just *rolled* it over there!"

That night, for the first time since Ma had died, Georgie and I ate dinner at the tavern. Oh, we had been to the Bent Pig often enough to help Pa stumble home, but not as paying customers, and definitely not to eat. Georgie and I sat beneath a kerosene lantern at a table in the back, eating from large bowls filled with pork, potato, and butter-bean stew, one of the Pig's specialties.

The bar was fairly crowded that night—fifteen to twenty men drinking and smoking and discussing the weather, their harvest, news from the city. Pa was buying drinks for friends and talking loud as usual, filling the room with his big booming voice. We could hear him all the way back at our table. He was bragging about his boys.

I looked over at Georgie. He was eating steadily but never taking his eyes off Pa, a big grin on his face. For my part, I couldn't shake the feeling that something was about to go wrong. Pa could hold his liquor, but sooner or later he would always reach a point when something slipped and suddenly he'd be soused. He already had more than a good start on it when we arrived, and I was worried. If he shot off his mouth about that boulder . . .

My apprehension shot up several notches as I saw Abe McClintock stomping through the door. His two huge sons, Caleb and Jake, were in tow. From the expression on Abe's face, I knew the mood in the Bent Pig was about to change.

Abe stopped inside the doorway, his thick callused hands perched on his hips. "John Neuman! Where the hell are you?" he bellowed, surveying the room as if he owned it. Caleb and Jake stood behind him like pit bulls, all muscle and spoiling for a fight.

Pa turned slowly. "You lookin' for me, Abe?"

"Damn right I am. Get that rock off my property!"

"What're you talking about?" Pa replied. "We put that stone dead center on the boundary wall, just like all the others."

"It's hanging a good six feet onto my field!"

"No more'n it is onto mine, Abe," Pa pointed out pleasantly. "If you don't approve of where it is, why don't you get those two strapping boys of yours move it?"

"Damn you, Neuman. There's no way we can move that rock."

"Why not? Me and *my* boys rolled it over there," Pa chuckled, clearly enjoying himself. "You telling me you McClintocks ain't up to it?"

Abe's face reddened. "My boys can outwork them skinny brats of yours any day of the week," he said. "Besides, you never rolled that stone. There's no track in the field."

"Well, Abe, it must've been nigh on dark when you went up there," said Pa. "Could be you just missed the track. Or," he added slyly, "maybe we raked over the ground so's you couldn't tell how we done it."

A number of Pa's cronies snickered, which was all the encouragement Pa needed. My bad feeling got worse. Pa didn't know when to quit.

"I'm telling you me and my boys moved that rock, and it's sitting in the middle of the north field to prove it," Pa taunted. "You may not like it, Abe, but that's a fact. And I'll tell you something else. That's rock's gonna stay right where it is because when it comes right down to it, none of you McClintocks is a match for a Neuman."

"That so?" McClintock's eyes turned squinty-shrewd. "If you're so sure of that, let's put some money on it."

Pa stroked his chin. "What've you got in mind?"

"What I have in mind is a wager, Neuman," Abe spat. "I've got money says my boys can wrestle them two runts of yours flat on their backs inside of five minutes."

The room quieted, the mention of money getting everyone's attention. I pushed away from my food. I wasn't hungry anymore.

29

At first Pa didn't reply. He knew he'd been backed into a corner. I could see it in his eyes, and I knew he was trying to figure a way out.

McClintock kept pushing, not giving Pa room to back out. "What's the matter, John?" he taunted. He reached into his pouch and slammed two gold coins on the bar. "You say your boys moved that rock? Hell, they shouldn't have any trouble with a couple McClintocks, then. Or maybe you were just shooting off your mouth, as usual."

Finally Pa spoke. "Even money?"

"Even money."

"You've got a bet."

That was just like Pa. He figured it was better for Georgie and me to take a beating than to back down himself. Seething, I watched as he tossed down his drink and ordered another. I could see his face in the mirror. He looked mad and sick and stubborn, all at the same time.

After finishing his fresh drink in one gulp, Pa turned and peered unsteadily into the smoky room. Then, wiping his mouth on his sleeve, he walked back to where Georgie and I were sitting.

"Thanks, Pa," I said when he arrived. "Thanks a whole lot."

"Button your lip, Seth." Pa pulled up a chair and sat with his back to the room, facing Georgie and me. Georgie was still eating.

"Listen, boys," Pa whispered, lowering his voice so's only we could hear. "I'll be damned if I'm gonna lose this bet to old man McClintock. Here's what I want you to do. Seth, you're smaller'n Georgie, so Jake'll probably take you. Keep away from him as long as you can. He'll get you, but make him work for it."

"Great plan," I said, shaking my head in disgust.

"Georgie, Caleb's gonna go for you," Pa continued, ignoring my sarcasm. "I want you to use that power of yours to keep from gettin' beat."

I couldn't believe my ears. "Pa, no!"

Pa glared. "Seth, you shut the hell up!" Then, to Georgie, "Can you use that power of yours just a little, so's nobody can tell? Just enough so's he can't beat you?"

Georgie seemed confused. "I . . . I guess so."

"Pa, it's not worth it," I said.

Pa was close to drunk by then, but still plenty quick. In a blink he backhanded me across the face. I didn't even have time to flinch. "I told you to shut up," he barked, slurring his words. "Don't make me tell you again, boy."

My face stung like fire, but I looked him straight in the eye. "It's not worth it."

"You'll do what I tell you," he warned, his voice laden with menace. "Georgie, you know what to do?"

"Yes, Pa. Don't let him beat me."

"Right." Pa rose from the table and clapped Georgie on the back, then turned to me. "We'll show them bastards. Right?"

I didn't say anything, glad Ma wasn't there to look into my heart and see what I was feeling. Pa glowered another warning at me, then stumbled back to the bar. Georgie finished his stew.

Within minutes a group of men had cleared the center of the room—stacking chairs against the walls and pushing tables to the corners—forming an open area in the middle. Extra lanterns were hung so there would be plenty of light. Men stood expectantly around the perimeter, waiting for things to begin.

Pete Jenkins was bartending that night. He agreed to hold the wagers, keep time, and settle any disputes. Although in his stubborn pride Pa had foolishly given Abe even odds, most side bets in the room were weighed heavily in favor of the McClintocks. Just about everyone had money down, and you could feel the tension mounting as Georgie and I stepped forward.

Jake and Caleb were already waiting. They had taken off their shirts so's not to get them torn. We did the same. As I said, Georgie was a big kid for nineteen, but Jake had twenty pounds on him, and Caleb was even bigger than that. Next to them we looked puny.

31

The rules were simple: no kicking, biting, or gouging. Everything else was okay. Jake and Caleb had five minutes to put us on our backs, either wrestled down or knocked unconscious. From the way the McClintock boys were grinning, I knew they intended the latter.

"Hey, swifty, c'mere," said Caleb, smacking his big-knuckled fist into his palm. "I've got somethin' for you."

"Aw, Caleb, you know my name's not swifty," Georgie replied with a smile.

"The match begins in thirty seconds," Pete yelled, staring at his pocket watch.

Balancing lightly on the balls of his feet, Jake squared off against me. "I'm gonna enjoy this," he said quietly.

"Fifteen seconds," Pete called, eyes still on his timepiece. "You boys ready?"

None of us said anything. I concentrated on Jake, watching his hands. The room had turned so still I could almost hear the blood pounding in my ears.

"Go!"

Jake charged in fast and low, trying to circle me with his arms. I sidestepped. As he went by I shoved down hard on his shoulders, slamming his face into the floor.

"Atta boy, Seth!" Pa hollered. "Now stay away from him."

Damn right, I thought.

Jake rose, blood streaming from his nose. He cupped his hand to his face, staring in disbelief as his palm filled with blood.

By now everybody was shouting. Old man McClintock yelled something at Caleb. Pa shifted to the other side and I could hear him yelling, too. A deafening mix of grunts and cheers and clamors resounded in the room, beating at me from all directions. Ignoring the roar, I focused on Jake.

Anger slowly replaced his look of surprise. I think he had planned to end it quickly by sweeping me off my feet. Now things had changed. I could see it in his eyes and the way he balled his fists. Now he wanted to hurt me. Bad.

I circled right, trying to keep space at my back so I would have room to move.

Jake charged a second time, swinging as he came in. I slipped his first punch and ducked inside, ramming my head into his face as hard as I could. Something crunched against my skull. I dropped to the floor and tried to roll away, but Jake got a grip on my ankle. I kicked and connected again. Jake loosened his hold. I twisted away and scrambled to my feet.

Jake was panting, his mouth spraying red with every breath. We were both spattered with blood. Jake's.

Abe screamed at Caleb. "Damn it, boy, finish him!"

Hearing this, I glanced over to see how Georgie was doing. Caleb was trying to wrestle Georgie down but couldn't seem to get a grip.

Without warning, Jake was on me. I never should have taken my eyes off him. He got his arms around me and lifted me off the floor and slammed me down on the wooden planks so hard I thought he'd broken my back. I couldn't move.

Dripping blood from his nose and mouth, Jake stood over me, eyes brimming with hate. Old man McClintock yelled something. Jake ignored him. With a snarl, he lifted his boot over my face and stomped down with all his might. I turned, taking most of the blow on my temple.

"No kicking!" yelled Pete.

Ignoring him, Jake used his boot again, catching me in the ribs. The blow lifted me off the floor. My head was ringing. I couldn't breathe. I lay helpless, retching.

Jake's lips curled in a grotesque red grimace. Reaching down, he grabbed my hair and jerked me up. I saw him cock his fist.

"Damn it, Jake, he's down!" Abe shouted, bursting into the circle and shoving his son aside. "Go help your brother!"

Reluctantly, Jake left me puking and hurried over to Caleb.

Eventually I got my breath. The spots before my eyes cleared. I rolled over and peered across the room.

Somehow Georgie was still up, even though both Caleb and Jake were now trying to bring him down. Everybody was yelling. Pa and Abe were shouting at each other—Pa contending two against one wasn't fair, McClintock arguing that it was. Pete called out the time. There were still two minutes to go.

I could see what Georgie was doing. He wasn't throwing any punches. He was just trying to stay on his feet, and he was using his "skin" to do it—employing it occasionally to break a hold or slip a punch. I smiled, recollecting just how slippery that "skin" was. Nonetheless, Georgie was having a tough time keeping track of both the McClintocks at the same time. One would approach from the front while the other threw a punch from behind. Some of them were landing. Georgie was getting tired.

Most in the room had money on the McClintocks, so naturally they were cheering for Caleb and Jake. The mood of frustration turned ugly as the final seconds slipped by. At one point Caleb and Jake piled on Georgie together, slid down his "skin," and wound up sprawled at his feet. If you didn't know what was happening, you'd have thought they were clowning around. Abe was furious.

Pa was laughing, catcalling the McClintock boys, mocking them.

Caleb and Jake didn't like getting laughed at any more than they liked getting beat. They looked ready to explode.

In a fight, five minutes is a long time. Nearly exhausted, the McClintock boys made one last run at Georgie, closing from opposite sides. It seemed as if Georgie just put out his hand and brushed Caleb aside, then neatly sidestepped Jake. Once again they wound up sprawled on the floor. Above all the shouts of anger and derision, I could hear Pa laughing.

"Time!" Pete yelled. "John Neuman wins the wager."

"Hold on," Abe shouted. "Jake got the younger one down. That makes it a draw."

Pa stopped laughing. "The bet was you'd get *both* my boys down. One ain't both."

At that point everyone with a money interest began voicing his opinion. I was fed up with the whole thing. Georgie started over to join me, a big grin on his face. He knew he'd done good.

Georgie was almost there when I saw Caleb sneaking up behind him, his eyes blazing with fury. Caleb had a wooden stool from the bar clenched in both hands.

"Georgie, look out!" I screamed.

Too late.

Caleb slammed the stool down on Georgie's head. I heard a sickening thud as the heavy oak stool connected with Georgie's skull.

The next few moments seemed like a horrible nightmare. It was as if a noiseless explosion suddenly detonated in the bar . . . with Georgie at the center.

Caleb was the closest. He got hit the hardest. It looked like an invisible fist just picked him up and hurled him across the room. And he wasn't the only one. Every man there got knocked flat, as did several walls near the kitchen. The front door was ripped from its hinges and blasted into the street. Every bottle behind the bar shattered, sending glass flying everywhere.

I was close to Georgie when it happened. I think what saved me was that I was partially shielded by a heavy support post, but I was still slammed to the floor. Hard. Shakily, I rose to my knees.

The room was silent. All the lanterns had been blown out. A few lay on the floor leaking kerosene. Luckily nothing caught fire. There was only one light left shining.

Georgie.

He lay unconscious, jerking like a poleaxed steer. As I watched, his back arched and his head began thrashing from side to side, as though he were fighting some unseen hand. There was something else, too. Georgie was floating a foot above the floor. *And he was glowing.*

"Oh, Georgie," I whispered.

Then it started.

"God save us!"

"Lord Jesus, what is it?"

"It's the work of the Devil!"

"Kill it!"

"Abomination!"

"Satan!"

I tried to crawl over to my brother. I couldn't get closer than a couple feet. That "skin" was all around him again, glowing, with him twisting and shuddering inside it.

Someone got a lantern lit, then another. Soon there was enough light to see the extent of the damage to the room. The Bent Pig was a shambles, but there was a worse damage than that. Caleb's lifeless body lay crumpled at the foot of the bar, a section of the stool he'd swung at Georgie buried in his chest.

"Oh, God, my boy," Abe sobbed, sinking down beside him.

"Jesus," Pa whispered.

"Georgie didn't mean it. It wasn't his fault," I said, stumbling over. Men shrank back as I approached. "It wasn't his fault," I repeated. "Tell them, Pa."

Abe rose to his feet and grabbed Pa's shirt. "What do you know about this, Neuman?"

Pa glanced away. "I don't know anything. You can't—"

A hollow thump sounded in the center of the room. Every man there turned. Georgie had dropped to the wood planking. The light around his body was gone.

With a snarl, McClintock released Pa and strode to the middle of the room. He stood over Georgie. "Get a rope," he said.

Pa stepped forward. "Now, hold on, Abe. You can't—"

Abe whirled, trembling with rage. "You shut your mouth. You got no right to speak. My boy's dead, and this . . . this *thing* you raised killed him. You keep out of this, Neuman, or I swear by all that's holy we'll be getting two ropes instead of one."

The wager money was still on the bar. I scooped it up. "Here," I said, thrusting it at Abe. "Take it. It wasn't Georgie's fault. Just take the money and leave us be."

Jake was standing beside me. He knocked the coins from my hand. Then he swung his fist, putting all his weight behind the blow. I went down. Hard. I wound up on the floor beside Caleb's body, blood pouring from my mouth.

Jake spat on me. "This ain't about the money," he said. "This is about right and wrong."

Someone brought a rope from the storeroom. With a hollow feeling, I realized that the men in that bar were going to hang Georgie, and there was nothing Pa or I could do to stop it. Rising to my knees, I looked up at my neighbors. All I could see in their faces was cruelty and fear and hate. They had changed. They had turned into a mob. Alone, each may have been fair and honest and moral; together, they had become an ugly mindless force bent on violence and revenge.

Rough hands jerked Georgie to his feet. They bound his wrists behind his back with wire. He was still dazed but starting to come out of it.

Abe dragged him to the bar, forcing him to look at Caleb's body. "You done this!" he hissed. "And by God, you're gonna pay."

Confused, Georgie stared down at Caleb, then peered around the demolished room. Slowly, he understood what had happened. As he did, I saw despair fill his eyes.

"It wasn't your fault, Georgie," I said.

Georgie looked down. "Yes, it was, Seth. I should have kept my promise to Mama."

I moved closer. "Listen to me," I said softly so only he could hear. "They're going to hurt you, Georgie. You have to save yourself, like when the boulder rolled on you."

"No, Seth," he said sadly. "I was wrong to do it. I'm not gonna do it any more."

"Please, Georgie," I begged.

"No."

I tried to think of something to convince him. I failed. And then the time for pleading was over. For then the men in the bar, that mob of men—my neighbors, my townsfolk, my friends— dragged my brother outside and threw a rope over the old maple by the bridge and put Georgie on Phil Johnson's mule and hung him.

I left Pa in the bar and stood in the woods, deep in the shadows. I saw it happen. All of it. I wanted to look away, but I couldn't. I kept praying Georgie would save himself, use his power just one more time. He didn't, at least not till the very end. And by then it was too late.

Nineteen men stood in the moonlight around the maple tree that night, laughing, watching Georgie kick. Watching him die.

Nineteen men.

Hate grew within me, swelling until it was all I could feel. It flooded through me like a venom, filling me till I thought I would burst. I could taste it. I wanted them to die. And all at once I knew how to do it. I wasn't able to solve the puzzle of Ma's cancer. No, I couldn't do it for love. The hours I'd spent beside her searching for a key to unlock the secret of her disease had been fruitless. But I did it for hate. A few minutes of hate and I had the answer.

In a dim part of my mind I wondered what sort of person I was. In another, I didn't care. I hungered for revenge. It drove me down to that circle of men. Unnoticed, I walked among them, pausing beside each. I didn't have to touch them; I just needed to be close. It didn't take long. And it was easy.

I planted the seeds deep, sowing them in their spines, their ribs, the long hollow bones of their legs. I placed the seeds where they would germinate slowly, then grow and mature and blossom into an agonizing death for each.

Afterward I returned to the woods, hot bitter tears running down my face. I cried for Ma. I cried for Georgie. I guess I cried for myself, too.

Hours later, after the moon had set and the men were gone, I cut Georgie down. Using a wheelbarrow from the livery stable, I wheeled him up to the north field. Then I returned home, got a shovel, and buried Georgie beside the boulder—figuring that rock he'd moved was better than any headstone I could have placed.

Afterward I sat under the stars, leaning against Georgie's boulder and thinking about what had happened. I decided Ma had been telling the truth in that story of hers. The men in the bar had been afraid of Georgie because he was different, and their fear had turned to hate, and their hate had destroyed him. I suspected that Ma had changed the ending of her story, though. I don't believe there ever was any cleansing rain for that monkey. I think that tribe of his tore apart their furry green brother and left him to die. And as Ma had said, that's just the way things were.

But if that was the way of the world, why would God burden my brother with a curse like that? Why would God make Georgie different just so his fellow men would kill him? What had my brother done to deserve such a heartbreaking, lonely end?

And what about me, and what I had done to the men who hung him? They deserved the fate I had given them, and I was glad I'd done it. But deep down I knew it was wrong. If there is a Creator, what will His judgment be for me? I wondered. Abruptly, I realized that He had *already* damned me, for I was different, too. I was green, just like that monkey . . . at least on the inside. Or was the color of my soul actually black?

Absently, I wondered if there were others like me—normal on the outside but different nonetheless. If there were, and they were still alive, I knew they would be hiding. I also knew I would never find them. But for some reason, at that moment, I wanted very much to believe they were there.

I remained in the north field all that night, sitting beside Georgie's boulder until the first light of dawn. By then it had turned bitter cold. The freezing air had stiffened my joints. I was sore from the fight as well. It took me a while just to stand.

The path lay in shadow as I followed it to the river. Standing on the bank in the early morning light, I watched the dark waters flow by. I stripped off my clothes and dived in. The river was icy cold and running fast. I swam out from shore, my arms slashing the surface, feeling the current trying to pull me down. When I began to grow numb, I stopped and let myself sink, descending into the frigid darkness. Shafts of sunlight streamed down from above, eerie fingers fanning through the depths. I hung weightless, wondering how it would feel to simply fill my lungs with one final watery breath.

Would I find peace? I wondered.

I doubted it.

When I burst gasping to the surface, I found that the current had carried me a considerable distance downstream. I was shivering when I reached the bank, but by then a morning breeze had come up, and I was dry by the time I found my clothes. I dressed and headed back to the cabin.

Pa was asleep when I arrived. Quietly, I gathered my things. There wasn't much—some clothes, a buckskin wallet Georgie had made for me, a locket of Ma's, my Grandpa's watch. They hardly filled my duffel bag. When I was done, I stood at the foot of Pa's bed. It looked half empty without Ma in it. Pa still slept on his side.

"Pa. Wake up."

"Huh?"

"Wake up, Pa."

Pa opened his eyes. I saw them cloud with shame as he remembered what had happened. Slowly, he swung his feet to the floor, rubbing a hand across the rough white stubble covering his chin. He still had on his clothes from the night before. A jar of liquor sat on the night table. He reached for it.

"Don't, Pa."

He peered over, seeming to notice me for the first time. Again, he ran a hand over his chin, then glanced at the jar.

"Please don't, Pa."

"No, I don't guess I will," he sighed, cradling his head in his hands.

"I buried Georgie in the north field by that boulder. I figure he'd have liked that."

"I think maybe he would," Pa said softly. Painfully, he rose from the bed. He looked old. Funny, I had never noticed it before. With a start, I realized that my father had grown old.

He stood unsteadily, trying to straighten. Then he spotted my bag by the door. "You're leaving?"

I nodded.

Pa's throat started working. I knew he had words to say. "Seth, I need to tell you something," he said quietly. "Will you listen?"

I didn't respond.

"Before your mother died, she made me promise to take care of you and Georgie after she was gone," he went on. "I told her of course I would; she didn't need me to promise. But she made me promise anyhow. And she made me promise something else," he added, his voice breaking. "She made me promise to love you."

I could see the torment in his face, but still I said nothing.

"Seth, I tried to do right by you both," he continued, fighting for control. "I swear I tried, but after Ma died, I . . . I don't know what happened. I know I failed you, just like I failed with everything—the plans I had for this farm, and how I was gonna send you and Georgie to school downriver, and . . ."

Pa's words trailed off. He swallowed hard, then pushed on. "Seems like only yesterday your mother and I stood before the preacher, with little Georgie already on the way. I was young then, not much older than you, full of plans and dreams. Guess that's all they were. Dreams. When Ma died, she took 'em with her."

He stepped closer, his eyes brimming. "I know you blame me for what happened. I know you hate me, boy. But Seth, I done the best I could."

Outside, I could hear the wind moving through the trees. The sun had crested the hill in back and was filtering through the window onto the worn planks at my feet. It was time to go. "I'll be leaving now," I said.

Pa's shoulders sagged. "I don't reckon I'll see you again."

"No, Pa. I reckon not."

"Well, so long, son," he said softly.

"Good-bye, Pa."

I picked up my duffel and left the cabin where I had spent the first fifteen years of my life. I walked down the dirt road to Auger's Crossing, and when I got to the river, I headed downstream and kept on going.

I never looked back.

*   *   *

I awoke slowly. Sunlight streamed into the stall, lighting the straw with a warm yellow glow. Breathing in the sweet scent of alfalfa, I lay quietly, listening to the sounds of the waking farm. Sandy's mare whinnied in the next stall, kicking impatiently for her morning feed. The cows' lowing told me they needed attention too, and I heard the chickens already scratching in the yard.

I rubbed my eyes. Sitting up, I spotted Christy Sullivan standing in the doorway. From her expression, I knew she had prepared herself for the worst.

"Good morning, Mr. Neuman," she said.

"Morning, Christy."

She took a deep breath. "Mr. Neuman, is Lucky—"

Before I could answer, Lucky shook off his blanket and let out a big, happy yelp.

"Mr. Neuman, you fixed her!' Christy squealed, running to her dog.

"Yeah, honey, I did. It'll be some time before he's walking again, but he's gonna be all right."

I got a good feeling watching the two of them together— Christy kneeling in the straw talking nonsense to Lucky, Lucky licking any bare skin on his master he could reach. Then, with a puzzled frown, Christy studied her dog for almost a full minute, her eyes fixed on him intently. Then she turned to me.

Something about her abruptly changed. Curious, I searched her eyes, again noticing that they were a deep, deep blue shot through with tiny flecks of gold. With a shock, I realized I had been right the day before. They *were* just like Ma's.

Though I tried, I couldn't look away. Time seemed to stop. I felt something shifting inside my head. All at once memories began flashing past my mind's eye: Ma. The boulder. Georgie's death. What I had done for Lucky. Everything.

Christy and I stared at each other, lost in the shock of recognition. A chill ran through me. Christy was different, too. In some strange way she was just as different as I, and she knew about me as well. She knew what I had done, all of it, and what it had cost me.

Without a word, Christy put her arms around my neck and gave me a hug. Somehow, for me, that hug was like Ma's cleansing rain. For the first time since Georgie's death I knew that I wasn't alone, and that there was someone I could trust. Then I felt something break inside me, shatter like ice on a pond, and with blinding clarity I saw the terrible burden of hate I had given myself to carry, and I realized what it had done to me.

Shaken, I walked to the window and leaned on the sill. At the foot of the pasture I could see a sliver of river glittering through the cottonwoods. The trees had just begun to show spring's first promise of green, and the air had a snap to it, crisp and clean. I stood for a long time. Finally I knew what I had to do.

There were others like Christy and me, and somehow I would find them. But first I had to return to Auger's Crossing. There were things there to set right. A lot of things. I didn't know whether I could, but while some of the men I had cursed still lived, I knew I had to try. And there was something else I had to do in Auger's Crossing as well. There was an old man there who lived in a cabin by the river. I had to see him one more time.

I stood a few moments longer, gazing across the valley. At last I turned back to Christy. She had rejoined Lucky and was sitting beside him in the straw, cradling his head in her lap. I felt a surge of satisfaction, knowing I had told her the truth. It would take months, but in the end her pup would be all right.

And with luck, and in time . . . so would I.

I Can't Sleep

Ever think about killing yourself? No, of course not. The world's been good to you. You're not ready to check out yet. Never even considered it, right?

Yeah, sure.

Well, let's suppose, just for the sake of argument, that you *did* want to take your own life. You have incurable cancer, say, and you're in intractable pain. Or you've suffered a stroke or been in a car accident and can't move a muscle, ever again. Or you're clinically depressed and getting through each and every day is a crushing, hopeless nightmare. Use your imagination and come up with your own scenario; the world has plenty of cruelties to dish out. If you're truthful, no matter who you are, you'll admit that there is a point past which life is no longer worth living. Believe me . . . I know.

So, given the foregoing, here's question number two: How would you do it?

Ideally, dying should be quick and painless, right? No argument there. Quick and painless. Unfortunately, those two words cover a lot of ground. For instance, if you do it properly, sucking the end of a twelve-gauge shotgun and thumbing the trigger is probably painless. It's also quick, although it has the disadvantage of being a bit messy. So is sitting in a tub of warm water and letting your blood slowly seep from a razored artery, but there's an intrinsic difference (besides the tub cleaning up with the mere pull of the plug) between the two. With the former you're suddenly . . . *gone*; with the latter you have time to consider the consequences of your final act, to fully appreciate those penultimate moments of approaching death.

On our last night together, those were options I gave my friend Holden Carr. Instant death with a bullet to the head, or the delayed experience of a long drop to the pavement.

His choice.

I'll never forget the look on his face. At the time I recall thinking that his nasty attitude about the situation was completely unrealistic. In retrospect I can understand it, but I still don't think he was being fair. Especially considering what he had planned to do to me.

My name is John Starling, and I'm an insomniac. Sounds like something you'd hear at an AA meeting, right? Okay, alcoholism is a serious problem, but in my book it doesn't come close to insomnia. For me there is no support group, no meetings, no sponsor to help me through the rough spots, no twelve-step, one-day-at-a-time approach to recovery. There *is* a bright side, though. Because of my affliction I've become an extremely wealthy man. But sometimes, in the early hours of morning, I can't help but think that if I had been able to sleep, perhaps Holden would still be alive.

It started about five months ago. I'm a swimming-pool contractor. Maybe you've heard of me. Starling Pools, Inc. I work the Las Vegas/Clark County area—mostly residential, but I've done some big jobs for the hotels as well. I like my work. Nonetheless, as with any occupation, there's stress. Goes with the territory. So when I began having trouble sleeping, I figured that's what it was. Stress.

I was wrong.

Missing a little sleep doesn't sound like much, does it? Well, at first it wasn't. I've always been able to get at least seven or eight hours of shuteye every night. It was something I took for granted—like the sun coming up in the morning or subcontractors trying to screw me—so when I unexpectedly found that all I could manage was two or three hours a night, I told myself it was temporary. Stress-related. Whatever.

I cut down on coffee. Then I stopped drinking caffeine entirely. At night I tried warm milk, sleeping pills, exercise, hot baths, pot, even reading *Scientific American*. Things got worse. Soon it wasn't just a *little* sleep I was missing. It was all of it.

In time I didn't even bother going to bed. Instead I stayed up watching late-night TV, hoping I would get bored enough to nod off for a few hours on the couch. We have a big ranch-style home (patio and pool out back, of course) just off Washington Street, and the TV in the den was far enough from our bedroom that I didn't have to worry about disturbing my wife, Sarah, who has *no* trouble sleeping. After a while I didn't care what I watched—old movies, CNN news, The Weather Channel, talk shows—not to mention the mind-numbing commercials for hits-from-the-sixties records (not available in any store!), fast-food, Ginsu knives. Sometimes after the sign-off I would just sit and stare at the snow on the screen. I read once that the "snow" you get on a dead TV channel is actually the visual signature of the cosmic background radiation, an electromagnetic remnant of the Big Bang. People the world over have been gazing at TV snow for years, thinking nothing of it. Then in the sixties two guys do a simple experiment and figure out what it is. Voilà! Nobel Prize. But that's the way life is. You can look at something all your life and never see it for what it really is.

One morning Sarah padded into the den, her auburn hair fetchingly disheveled from sleep. "John, you look awful," she said, leaning down to kiss me. "You can't go on like this, honey. You're seeing Dr. O'Brien today," she added, her voice slipping into its no-nonsense mode.

I flipped off the TV. "Can't. Got meetings this morning and a full afternoon." Wearily, I ground my fists into my eyes. "I'll be okay."

"Absolutely not. Call your office and have someone else take care of things," she said, her partially open terrycloth robe revealing her long dancer's legs. Even first thing in the morning she looked great.

"But—"

"No buts. You're going to see Dr. O'Brien today, and that's that. I'll have the girls work you into the schedule."

When I first met Sarah she was a featured dancer in a feather show at the Tropicana. I noticed her right off. Aside from being the most gorgeous woman I had ever seen, she could dance. I couldn't take my eyes off her. She has a distinctive way of carrying herself, a physical presence I can spot across a room—

the way she stands, the set of her shoulders, the tilt of her head. We started going out. Six months later we were married. Sarah quit the show, got a job as a medical assistant, and before long she moved up to the front office. She has a knack for computers and a flair for organization, and within a year she had become the office manager for the medical corporation of Jenkins, Gilbert, and O'Brien. Beauty *and* brains. I was a lucky guy, and I knew it.

Sitting in the den, I knew from Sarah's expression that there was no use arguing. Anyway, she was right. My office runs just fine without me. Besides, I hadn't been worth a damn at work since I stopped sleeping. Sometimes I would be sitting at my desk and realize I had no recollection of what had happened for the past thirty minutes. It was time to get help.

So promptly at ten-fifteen that morning I shuffled into the office of Jenkins, Gilbert, and O'Brien. Following a short wait, a nurse ushered me into an examining room. Moments later Dr. O'Brien entered, flipping through my chart on the way in. Dr. O'Brien was short, stout, and missing most of his hair. I had met him several times at office parties I'd attended with Sarah.

"Hello, John," he said. "Your wife tells me you're having trouble sleeping."

"That's putting it mildly," I grumbled. "Truth is, I haven't been sleeping at all."

"Oh, I seriously doubt *that*," he said with a knowing smile. "The human body can't go without sleep for more than a few days."

As near as I could tell, I hadn't slept in a week . . . not counting those blank periods at work.

"You've probably been catching catnaps here and there that you don't remember," he continued pleasantly. "Had any stress lately?"

"No."

"You're sure?"

"I'm sure," I snapped. Dr. O'Brien's cheery attitude was beginning to bug me.

"Okay, John," he said, settling his considerable bulk on the edge of the examining table. "Insomnia's a fairly common occurrence. Most people experience it at one time or another, and it's usually temporary." His reassuring voice had taken on a pedantic, singsong tone, and I had to struggle to appear properly attentive.

"Some people can get by on a few hours a night," he droned on. "Others need as many as ten. There's a big range, you see, but the main cause of insomnia is usually anxiety and stress. I'm going to prescribe a drug that should help you relax and get you back on track. Take two before bedtime," he added, handing me a hastily scribbled prescription.

"What is it?" I asked suspiciously, trying to decipher his writing.

"It's a drug that relieves anxiety and promotes sleep."

"What if it doesn't?"

"Oh, I suppose we could try another drug. At that point we would probably also consider doing a complete workup—blood, EEG, CAT scan—to rule out any organic etiology. Maybe get a neurologic consult as well, perhaps a psychiatric evaluation." Smiling, Dr. O'Brien rose from the table. "But I don't think that will be necessary. Make an appointment for next week. We'll see how you're doing then."

I got the drift: Get better, John . . . or else.

I set up an appointment for the following Thursday, but I never kept it. By then I didn't care.

By then the visions had started.

On the way home from Dr. O'Brien's, I made several stops— one to fill my prescription, another to pick up food at the market. We had invited Holden over for dinner that night, and although I didn't feel like company, it was too late to cancel. As I shopped, I abruptly realized that people were staring at me. Though I never caught them, I could feel their accusing eyes following me as I passed shoppers in the aisles. I got out of there as quickly as I could. All the way home I kept wondering the same thing: *What was happening to me?*

That night Holden knocked on our door at around seven. "Hi, guys," he said, strolling in and punching me lightly on the shoulder, then giving Sarah a kiss. I'd met Holden in college; we had played football together at the University of Arizona and been friends ever since. Holden was big, even bigger than I am, and solidly built. He had kept himself in shape, although lately I'd detected what looked like the beginnings of a paunch.

"I want you to meet somebody," Holden continued, proudly placing an arm around his date—a willowy young thing named Sandee who was short on brains and long on looks. Definitely Holden's type. Sandee cocktailed the late shift at the MGM Grand and had to be at work at eleven, so we got right down to drinks.

Since my problem began, I hadn't been able to drink. Not much, anyway. One or two cocktails hit me hard, and I would spend the rest of the evening trying not to slur. I nursed a beer until we sat down to dinner.

Sarah outdid herself that night: Caesar salad, seafood pasta with shrimp, scallops, and clams in a spicy red sauce, hot garlic bread, and tiramisù for dessert. I think she was unconsciously trying to get our lives back on track with that meal. I wasn't hungry. Nonetheless, the evening went well until Holden started expounding his gambling theory. Sarah and I had heard it before; his performance was obviously for Sandee's benefit. Mumbling something about helping to clear the table, I excused myself, grabbed some dishes, and followed Sarah into the kitchen. As I began rinsing plates, I found myself listening to Holden's explanation in the next room, begrudgingly admitting that despite his didactic tone, my friend did have a few things to say about gaming. Holden was a professional gambler.

"Why does the average Joe leave the tables a loser?" Holden began, talking around a mouthful of tiramisù. Then, answering his own question, "Simple. It's because he plays till he loses. The house has the resources to hang in while he's winning, so if the guy keeps playing—and they all do—sooner or later he's gonna lose. And when that happens and he's lost the farm and then some, he's forced to quit. The house just has to wait him out."

"So how do *you* do it?" wide-eyed Sandee asked as Sarah and I returned for more dishes.

"Simple. I quit when I'm ahead," Holden replied. "I only play craps, which is as close to even odds as you can get, and every day, rain or shine, I place a five-hundred-dollar bet on the pass line. If I win, I walk away a winner."

"And if you lose?"

"Then I double the wager. If I lose again, I double the bet once more, and so on. I have enough to double-up ten times, but I've never had to go that far. And as soon as I win, I quit—ahead five hundred bucks every day I play. Tax free, too," he added slyly.

"Of course, it's not quite that simple," he went on after a moment, clearly pleased with Sandee's reaction. "If I pass the fifth repetition, I exceed the single-bet limit of ten thousand dollars. But I have a way around that as well, and I've only had to go to the seventh roll once. It's foolproof. Know the chances of losing ten times straight?"

Sandee didn't have a clue.

I did. I had worked it out; it was about one in a thousand. I also knew where Holden got his backing. He'd taken out a $250,000 home-equity credit line years ago, and to my knowledge he had dipped into it deeply more than once. In my book, Holden was heading for a fall. I was coming back from the kitchen carrying a carafe of decaf when I suddenly tired of the subject.

"Enough about gambling," I said. "Why don't we talk about something—"

All at once I froze. I couldn't move. As if in a dream, I heard the coffee hit the floor.

"Honey, what's wrong?" Sarah cried. I heard her run in from the kitchen and felt her hands steadying me. I tried to speak, but couldn't.

Seconds ticked by. At last, the paralytic fist that had gripped me eased. Sarah helped me to a chair. I slipped into it gratefully, cradling my head in my hands.

"What the hell was *that*?" said Holden.

"John's been having trouble sleeping lately," Sarah answered, rubbing my neck. "Feeling better, hon?"

"No," I answered. God, I was tired.

"Hey, we've gotta be goin' anyway," said Holden, taking that as his cue to leave. "Sandee's shift starts in twenty minutes. Time I got to work, too. Thanks for dinner, Sarah." He kissed her, then gave me a thump on the back. "Take care of yourself, pal. Get some sleep."

Get some sleep. Sounded fine to me. If only it were that easy.

After they left I stumbled to the bathroom, grabbed my prescription vial, and shook out several of Dr. O'Brien's miracle pills. I inspected them doubtfully. *Were these small pills to be my salvation?* I wondered. I took two, as directed. Then I took two more for good measure.

That night Sarah and I made love. Afterward I stared at the insides of my eyelids until I heard her breathing turn soft and regular. Then I eased out of bed, made my way to the den, and turned on the TV. Not bothering to search for a station, I just sat gazing blankly at the TV snow. After a while I noticed something peculiar. Leaning closer, I peered at the screen. A chill ran through me. Reflected in the glass I could see myself in a smaller screen, where I was sitting before a yet smaller screen, and another, and another, and another . . .

The weird thing was—I was looking at my back.

I got Sarah's hand mirror. Holding it to one side, I checked the screen. The figure there was holding a mirror too, but now I could see his face in each smaller mirror.

It was me.

I rubbed my eyes, then peered again at my images. And as I watched, they changed. I saw my multiple selves in one of the casinos. I couldn't tell which casino it was, but knew I would recognize it if I saw it again. I was playing blackjack. And winning. Winning big.

Each blackjack hand was crystal clear, etched in my memory as if I had seen it many times before. I could make out the dealer, along with several other players. And there was someone else—a shadowy figure standing behind me. Although I tried, I couldn't see his face.

Once more the scene shifted and I was in a dark room surrounded by looming, unfamiliar objects. The shadowy figure from the casino crept up behind me. He raised something over his head. It looked like a knife. I wanted to scream a warning, but horror held me silent. I saw myself stagger and crumple to the floor, my hands trying to ward off the attacker's blows.

And God, oh, God, the blood.

I turned off the set and sat in the darkness until my heart stopped racing and my breathing returned to normal. *What had I seen? Had I glimpsed the future? Or had it simply been a waking nightmare, a result of my insomnia?*

I had to find out.

Without making a sound, I returned to the bedroom and dressed. Sarah was still tucked under the covers, curled comfortably around her dreams. How I envied her. On the way out I paused in the doorway, then reentered the room. From the top shelf of the closet I pulled down a small box. I opened it and took out a revolver that I had bought years earlier after my office was burglarized. It was a Smith & Wesson .38 Special with a four-inch barrel. It felt like a snake in my hand.

I inserted five copper-clad shells, leaving the first cylinder empty. I shoved the pistol into my belt at the small of my back. My coat covered it just fine. If what I'd seen hadn't been a hallucination, I planned on being prepared.

The green numerals on the dashboard of my car read three-thirty as I wheeled out of the driveway and headed downtown. The desert air was still sizzling and I opened all the windows, letting the hot drafts bathe my face. After passing McCarran Airport, I hung a right on Las Vegas Boulevard, wondering where to begin my search. Deciding one place was as good as the next, I pulled into the Dunes, left my car in the lot, and entered the casino. Right away I knew it was wrong. I left the Dunes and worked my way along the Strip, stopping at the Sands, the Desert Inn, the Stardust, Circus Circus, Bellagio, and the Riviera. No luck at any of those, either. I kept going. At around 5:00 AM, I arrived at the Hilton. When I pushed through the Hilton's heavy glass doors, I knew I had found it. It just felt . . . *right.*

Even that late, the casino was still busy—alarms announcing slots winners, keno girls hustling bets, players huddled around the tables, and everywhere the smell of alcohol, stale cigarettes, and sweat. I entered the casino, afraid that I was heading for trouble but unable to stop. I had to find out.

I slid onto a stool at a deserted hundred-dollar blackjack table. With a chill, I recognized the dealer. No doubt about it— he was the one I had seen in my vision. He gave me a bored look, then scooped up a fan of cards laid out on the felt and began a six-deck shuffle. I opened my wallet and placed four hundred dollars on the table.

Upon finishing his shuffle, the dealer offered me a stiff red card. After I cut, he dropped the decks into a shoe, converted my bills to a small stack of chips, and gazed over expectantly. "Place your bet, sir."

I hesitated, wanting to be wrong about what I'd seen in my den. But deep down, I knew I wasn't. I knew what cards would be coming up. I hadn't memorized them—I just knew.

With a feeling of dread, I pushed my whole stack onto the bet line. I hit on twelve and held on eighteen. The dealer stayed on seventeen. I let it ride, recalling that my next hand was going to be a natural—an ace and a queen.

It was.

I played on, placing minimum wagers on hands I knew I was going to lose, betting my whole stack on the winners. Before long I was playing the table limit. Twenty minutes later, when I realized I no longer knew what cards would be coming up, I quit. By then a small crowd had gathered behind me.

I counted my chips. Forty-two thousand dollars. "May I deposit this in a hotel account?" I asked, starting to sweat as I recalled the second part of my vision. Even though I could feel the reassuring weight of the pistol pressing into my back, I didn't want to leave with all that money, even in the form of a check.

"Yes, sir," the pit boss answered. He stepped forward from behind the dealer, where I had noticed him watching as soon as my bets hit the limit. "I'll have someone assist you," he added, signaling a security guard.

"Thanks." I slipped the dealer a thousand-dollar chip. "For the boys."

"Thank you, sir!" the dealer replied with a smile, tapping it on the table twice before dropping it into his shirt pocket.

It was still dark outside when I started for my car. On the way I suddenly had the feeling I was being followed. I heard footsteps behind me. I stopped. They stopped. I whirled.

Nothing.

I walked faster, certain I was approaching some horrible fate I couldn't avoid. Soon I was running. I could still hear him running behind me, getting closer. My breath coming in ragged gasps, I turned a corner and raced into the parking garage. Ahead I saw my car. Fighting an impulse to jump in and speed away, I ducked behind a concrete column.

I had to know.

Heart pounding, hands slippery with sweat, I pulled out the pistol. Whatever the cost, I decided to end things there and then. Holding the revolver at my side, I pulled the trigger once, hearing the hammer click on an empty cylinder. The next one held a live shell.

I intended to use it.

I held my breath as the footsteps approached, the gun heavy in my hand. I could smell my own sweat, sour and rancid. A figure appeared. I tried to raise the gun. With a shock, I discovered that I couldn't. I was frozen again, just as I had been earlier that evening. But this time I knew it wouldn't be just coffee that wound up getting spilled. It would be my blood.

Straining with every ounce of will I possessed, I struggled to raise the gun.

I couldn't move my hand . . . not even a millimeter.

Without as much as a glance in my direction, the shadowy figure moved on.

After he'd gone, I remained behind the concrete column, trembling uncontrollably. *Why had he spared me?* I asked myself. *Was he toying with me, tormenting me?*

Then another thought occurred. *Had I nearly made a mistake?* What if he had simply been an innocent passerby—a hotel employee, a garage attendant, a gambler leaving from a late-night stint at the tables?

No. I couldn't accept that. My vision in the TV screen had been no hallucination. The cards at the blackjack table had proved it.

*   *   *

"How'd you sleep last night, hon?" Sarah asked at breakfast later that morning. "The pills help?"

"Yeah," I lied. I couldn't tell her what I had seen in our TV, or what had happened at the Hilton. It was too much to grasp, even for me. And I had been there.

"Going to work today?"

"No. I think I'll stay home," I answered, my mind racing. *Why did she want to know?*

"Good. You still look tired." Finishing the last of her coffee, she checked the clock over the stove. "Jeez, I've gotta run. I'll call from the office during lunch and see how you're doing." Then, bending to kiss my cheek, "I'm worried, John. You going to be okay?"

"I'll be fine."

"I love you."

"Love you back," I mumbled.

That night I doubled Dr. O'Brien's dosage again, taking eight of the little pills. Nonetheless, as usual, I found myself wide-awake after Sarah had fallen asleep. Around midnight I got up and made my way to the den, going straight to a snowy channel on the TV. Once more I saw my multiple selves reflected in the surface of the television screen, just as I had the night before.

Time passed. My reflections started to move. Again, I saw myself at the blackjack table. As before, I knew each hand as if I had played it a hundred times. The shadowy figure was there too, close enough to touch. I still couldn't see his face. Knowing what was coming next, I was afraid to watch, but I couldn't tear my eyes away from the images in the screen.

Death at the hands of my loathsome nemesis came suddenly this time—violent, hideous, and bloody.

I had to go back to the Hilton.

What happened next is mostly a haze. I recall getting dressed, shoving the gun into my belt, slipping into my car. Of the trip downtown I remember nothing. My first clear recollection is of crossing the Hilton casino floor and approaching a five-hundred-dollar blackjack table. As I sat, the pit boss from the night before spotted me.

"Evening, Mr. Starling," he said, stepping behind the dealer.

I nodded, noting the nameplate on his coat. Frank. I wasn't surprised that he knew me; it was his job to recognize the players. And after last night, I was a player. "I have money on deposit," I said. "I'd like it all in large chips, please."

"Certainly." Frank made a call on the pit phone, returning with a marker for me to sign. Then the dealer assembled several stacks of chips before me—red-and-black hundreds, blue-and-gray thousands.

I began by betting the ten-thousand-dollar limit on hands I knew were winners, pulling back to five hundred on the losers. When my stacks got unwieldy I switched to the five-thousand-dollar chips. At that point the dealer closed the table to other players and security moved in to contain a crowd that had assembled behind me. Soon I was playing all five positions. On one single hand, when I knew the dealer was going to bust, I raked in fifty thousand dollars.

At the end of the shoe they changed dealers and brought out six new decks. I counted my winnings: nineteen stacks of five-thousand-dollar chips, ten per stack. I did the math. Almost a million, not counting my smaller chips.

I played on. Then something went wrong. I felt a prickling at the back of my neck. I could feel him behind me.

I glanced over my shoulder.

It was Holden.

"What . . . what are you doing here?" I croaked, barely able to speak.

"Sarah asked me to keep an eye on you," he answered. A lie. Sarah didn't even know I had been going out.

"So you *followed* me?"

"Not exactly," he answered guiltily. "It was easy enough to track you down, though. It's a small town."

"Cards, sir?" the dealer asked.

I turned back to the table, my mind spinning. I couldn't believe it. *Holden.* Numbly, I glanced at my hand.

It was all wrong, not the cards I had seen in the dream.

I could feel Holden's eyes boring into my back. I lost the next four hands. Rising shakily, I tipped the dealer a white-and-orange five-thousand-dollar chip. "Please credit my winnings to my account," I said.

"Yes, sir, Mr. Starling. And thank you."

Determined to confront Holden, I turned.

He was gone.

A security guard accompanied me to the cashier's office, where I was given a receipt for my winnings. Afterward the casino manager offered me a hotel suite, along with complimentary wine, food, companionship—anything I wanted. They didn't want me leaving. I didn't blame them. At that point I had over two million dollars of their money.

With a shrug, I accepted. *Why not?* I thought. I had nothing better to do. Besides, I was in no hurry to face the next part of my vision.

A bellhop escorted me to a penthouse on the twenty-ninth floor. The "Elvis" suite. After he'd gone, I locked the door and surveyed the well-appointed rooms—leather couches, surround-sound stereo, fully stocked bar, a big-screen TV. I avoided the

TV. Doors led to several bedrooms, each boasting a king-sized bed and a sweeping view of the Strip. All were empty. I checked.

Satisfied that I was alone, I stepped onto a private balcony just beneath the big red Hilton sign atop the building. Bathed in its glow, I stood by the balcony wall, breathing in the night air and staring at the casino lights on the streets below. I had been out there for some time when I heard a knock at the door.

It was Holden.

My heart tripping like a jackhammer, I let him in—never taking my eyes off him, not even for an instant. My mouth went dry. I still couldn't believe he was the one.

"You look like hell," Holden noted, lurching past me. I could smell the reek of bourbon on his breath.

Was he drunk, or just acting that way to put me off guard?

"How 'bout a drink?" he suggested, slurring his words.

"No, thanks," I answered, keeping my distance.

"Meant for me," he chuckled, staggering around to the business end of the bar.

When he turned toward me again, I had the gun in my hand.

"What the hell . . . ?"

"No more cat-and-mouse, Holden. Just tell me why. What did I ever do to you?"

He edged out from behind the bar. "C'mon, John. Quit kiddin' around."

"I'm not kidding, Holden. Tell me."

He spread his hands, trying to smile. "Hey, pal, you never did anything to me." He couldn't take his eyes off the gun.

"Then why do you want to kill me?"

"Kill you? I just came up to ask for a loan. Figured you could afford it, seein' how you just won big." He licked his lips. "Listen . . . forget the loan. Just put down the gun."

He had started to sweat. I saw a something in his eyes—fear, hate, maybe both. He glanced at the door as if he were expecting someone. Like a fool, I fell for it. As I looked over my shoulder, he rushed me. And at that moment I knew for sure—just as I had known what cards would be coming up in the casino. My nemesis was Holden.

I swung the pistol, connecting with the side of his head just above his left eye. He grunted and collapsed on the carpet, splayed out like a side of beef.

He was heavy. It took me several minutes to drag him outside and position him on the balcony wall. It was hard work, and I nearly lost him before getting him propped up in the corner just right. I was breathing hard when he came to.

"Jesus. What the . . ."

"Don't move," I ordered. "Not one inch. I'll shoot you right now if you do."

"What the hell are you doin'?" he said, his eyes wide with fear. I could tell he was about to make a move.

"Don't," I warned. "I know what you're planning. It has to end now. There's no other way."

Holden's eyes got even wider as I gave him his options: a quick and painless bullet, or the long drop behind him. His choice. It was the least I could do. After all, he had once been my friend.

He chose the bullet. "But let me do it myself," he begged, unable to hide the crafty look in his eyes. If I'd had any lingering doubts, that look dispelled it.

Holden was balanced precariously on the balcony wall, a thirty-story drop behind him. "Sure, *pal*," I said, handing him the gun and grabbing his ankles at the same time.

He leveled the pistol at me, just as I knew he would. "You're crazy!" he shouted, attempted to scoot his butt forward off the wall.

I lifted his ankles to keep him from moving.

"Don't make me shoot you!"

I lifted his feet even higher. He was close to going over. Panic filled his face.

"No!" he pleaded.

Then he pulled the trigger.

I heard the hammer click on the empty chamber. A live round was up next. Before he could pull the trigger a second time, I jerked his legs over his head. The gun clattered to the deck. "Good-bye, Holden," I said.

He screamed all the way down.

At the coroner's inquest I testified that Holden, drunk to the gills, had come up to the penthouse to borrow money. When I'd refused, he had climbed onto the balcony wall and threatened to jump. Of course at that point I had agreed to help him, but while climbing down he had accidentally slipped and fallen to his death.

A lie, but who would've believed the truth?

Oddly enough, it turned out that Holden actually *was* in financial trouble. That afternoon he had lost ten straight passes at the craps table. His luck had run out. Case closed.

Sarah convinced me to see Dr. O'Brien one more time. He put me on different pills. They even worked for a while, allowing me to get a few precious hours of sleep each night for almost a week. Then I had to double, triple, quadruple the dose. In the end they stopped working altogether.

Now I'm back in front of the TV again, watching my favorite show: cosmic background radiation, brought to you by the Big Bang. Night after night I see my reflection in the screen, watch myself die at the hands of the shadowy figure.

That's right.

My nemesis is back.

But now I know who it is.

I've had plenty of time to think, and I've realized a couple of things. I was wrong about Holden. I see that now. Oh, he wasn't innocent, not by a long shot. He was merely part of a more insidious plan.

Just like the cosmic background radiation, the answer was there all the time, staring me in the face. One night I finally saw it. Peering into the TV, I noticed something hauntingly familiar about my assailant. All at once I recognized that limber dancer's stance, the set of her shoulders, the tilt of her head.

Sarah.

I can't let on that I know what she and Holden were planning. I'll be pleasant to her at breakfast, call her at work during the day, lie beside her at night till she falls asleep. And I'll be very, very careful.

I know what I have to do. And when the time is right, I'll do it. I have plenty of time to plan, plenty of time to make certain everything is perfect.

Plenty of time.

Twenty-four hours a day. Every day.

As I said, I have a problem . . .

I can't sleep.

Final Exam

You will enter the (unintelligible) now.

The words thundered in my head, bouncing around inside my skull for what seemed like forever. "I'm not deaf, at least not yet," I shot back with as much sarcasm as I could muster. "You don't have to shout."

Actually, shouting doesn't come close to describing what they were doing. From the beginning, all of their commands had been delivered telepathically—the volume cranked up full and injected with maddening precision into my brain one syllable at a time, as if I were so stupid that everything had to be spelled out.

Fighting a wave of revulsion, I stared at the squirming thing on the deck—a glistening, sluglike cylinder around five meters long and two meters in diameter, with short slimy appendages studding its greenish-brown surface. At one end, an elliptical orifice opened and closed, winking at me like an obscene eye.

Enter now.

They had turned the volume down somewhat, but they were still spelling it out. I resented it like hell. No one likes being treated like an idiot, even if compared to them your IQ really *is* down in the amoeba range.

"What?" I asked aloud. Early on I had learned that they could read my thoughts, but I still hadn't grown used to just *thinking* at them.

Enter.

"Enter what?"

The (unintelligible)!

I smiled, sensing a hint of irritation. Early on I had also learned that resistance was futile. So far any order I disobeyed had quickly resulted in punishment something akin to sticking your head in a power conduit, only worse. But I couldn't stop myself. I have a stubborn streak a mile wide, and if they insisted on treating me like a moron—well, I figured on playing it to the hilt. Besides, I wanted to put off the inevitable for as long as possible.

Then the pain began, and I knew I couldn't hold out much longer. Soon, no matter how hard I fought, I would be crawling into that wet, gaping mouth.

Three days back I had been on the bridge of the *UFS Drake*, one of the last two-man surveyships still operational in the fleet. We were stationed in the third quadrant of a constellation known as the Dragon's Eye, orbiting NGC 11746915—a stellar binary that had recently turned into a particularly interesting subject for scientific study. The dual star system was composed of a small black hole circling a medium-sized G-type sun that had left the main sequence a million years back, swelling to a red giant. By gravitationally drawing a bridge of gas from the swollen primary, the black hole was gradually devouring its larger companion. In the process, it was releasing tremendous amounts of energy in the form of twin jets emanating from both poles of the singularity, along with intense radiation from the surrounding accretion disc.

We had been gathering data for just under two weeks when an alien spacecraft squeezed out of the black hole.

My first officer, Axle Chang, and I were on the observation deck at the time. Axle is short, with curly red hair, a razor-sharp mind, and a decidedly Irish temperament contrasting his otherwise Asian equanimity. An unusual combination, but Axle is an unusual guy. He can fix just about anything—be it atomic, electrical, mechanical, or photonic. You name it; Axle can make it work. A guy like him could mean the difference between life and death on an aging ship like the *Drake*, and I was lucky to have him.

"What the—" Axle bolted upright in his chair, spilling most of his coffee on the sensor console. "Captain, take a look at this!"

I leaned over Axle's shoulder, staring at the three-dimensional image in the screen. I tried to swallow, but couldn't.

Nothing is supposed to be able to escape the gravitational pull of a black hole. Nothing—not even light. The tidal effect created by just getting too close to a black hole is enough to rip ordinary matter to bits. "My God," I whispered. "Look at the size of it."

We looked.

Slowly, the craft oozed out of the singularity. The vessel looked like a huge, liquid-silver bubble and had to be at least a thousand kilometers in diameter, the size of a small moon.

"Are you recording this?" I asked, unable to control a quaver in my voice.

"Yes, sir," Axle answered, his hands a blur on the sensors.

Seconds later the alien ship emerged completely, lighting up the event horizon with a brilliant flash. Spellbound, we watched as it pulsed and shimmered, bolts of energy discharging from its surface. Then, without warning, it was beside us—not five hundred kilometers from the *Drake*. We never saw it move. It was suddenly just . . . there.

Axle rose from the command console and stumbled backward, his face ashen. "Cap, something's accessing our onboard computer. I don't know how, but I—"

It's hard to describe what happened next. One minute I was on the bridge, the next I found myself suspended in total, impenetrable darkness. I could feel nothing around me, not even the deck beneath my feet. With a sinking feeling, I began to suspect that I was no longer aboard the *Drake* . . .

Time passed.

My skin itched. My muscles twitched. Then thoughts and images began popping into my brain, flashing past as if someone were shuffling through my memories like riffling a deck of cards. "Hey!" I yelled. "Stop that!"

Actually, I tried to yell but couldn't. I had no control of my body. But I did *think* it, and someone got the message.

Cooperate or suffer punishment.

I had always imagined that direct mind-to-mind communication, if it existed at all, would be soft and tenuous and mystical, like whispering tendrils of thought insinuated into your consciousness. This *hurt*. "What . . . what are you doing," I demanded, screwing my eyes shut in concentration.

You are being examined. Afterward you will be tested.

"Tested for what?"

To determine whether your species is fit to join the brotherhood of servant races.

"You're slavers, eh?" I was scared but trying to maintain a good front, figuring people were the same the galaxy over. Give 'em an inch and they think they own you. "What if I don't want to join your so-called brotherhood?"

Irrelevant.

The response was accompanied by a searing bolt of pain that convinced me to keep my thoughts private, if possible. As I soon learned, it was not.

Their "examination" seemed endless. Occasionally they let me sleep, then woke me with a nudge of pain and began anew. Some of it wasn't bad, like reliving experiences I had long forgotten—life as a kid on Mars, my first flight in an antigrav harness, listening to my Granddad's stories about mining the asteroid belts—but for the most part what they did to me can only be described as a nightmare, a mental rape.

And then the real testing began.

Apparently using the same technique they had used to snatch me off the *Drake*, they shifted me to a glowing, cavernous chamber. Although the bright light in my new surroundings hurt my eyes, it felt good to be able to see once more. I had control of my body again, too. Squinting, I peered around the room. On all sides, luminous walls curved to a domed ceiling far above. The deck beneath my feet felt spongy and pliant, almost alive. Glowing a deep blood-red, a giant dodecahedral crystal sat in the center of the room atop a raised platform. Scattered around the crystal were peculiar-looking devices, many spouting tentacles and odd, jointed appendages.

No sign of my hosts.

Moments later I embarked on a battery of tests seemingly designed to determine my body's capabilities. They controlled my every move; I was just along for the ride. I strutted across the chamber, raising my heels high off the deck. I carried objects tiny and delicate, heavy and large. I operated alien machines, pushed buttons, pulled levers. Some tasks proved impossible, like manipulating devices that seemed more suited to someone with tentacles than fingers. Other tasks I performed easily. They subjected me to heat, cold, electric shock, taking everything to the extreme—how fast, how long, how much pain could I endure.

Somehow I lived through it. And in the end, I sensed that they considered me physically acceptable, if only marginally intelligent. But acceptable, nonetheless.

I felt miserable—not only from the testing, but because I realized that I had probably been instrumental in getting Homo sapiens into a world of trouble. Given the opportunity, I'd have simply dug in my heels and refused to be tested, or flunked on purpose, or whatever. I just never got the chance. Angrily, I wondered what they had planned for me next. Death? Or would I have the honor of joining their brotherhood as the first serving human?

Suddenly I heard a click. A section of bulkhead slid back, revealing a large recess.

An instant later it squirmed out.

I backed away in terror. Leaving a trail of slime, the thing on the deck slithered toward me, its hideous mouth opening and closing hungrily. "What the hell is *that*?" I croaked.

The (unintelligible) will complete your examination. Enter it now.

"Wait! What . . . what can you possibly learn from having that thing eat me?" I stammered, stalling for time.

Enter now.

I tried everything to avoid going in. Punishment is a great convincer, but I held out. After a while they lost patience, took control of my body, goose-stepped me across the chamber, forced me to my knees, and shoved my head into that horrible, slimy mouth.

A moment later I was in.

Paralyzed, I lay on my stomach in total darkness, steeling myself for the worst.

Nothing happened.

I groped around. The inky space surrounding me seemed inexplicably large. The surface pressing into my cheek felt coarse and gritty. Strangely, my hands encountered nothing out to the sides or above me. Briefly I considered trying to back my way out of the slug. I quickly gave up that idea, reasoning I would simply be forced to reenter. Besides, for some reason I couldn't locate the opening. Instead I sat, hugging my knees and shivering in the cold.

Minutes dragged by, turning to hours. Then slowly, almost imperceptibly, a faint light began building on a distant horizon.

Horizon?

To my amazement, an angry red sun rose slowly before me, firing the sky with oranges and golds. Rubbing my eyes in disbelief, I stared at my surroundings. Sparkling in the morning light, a blue-green ocean lay at my feet, small waves gently lapping its shore. To my right a dazzling white beach traced the water's edge to a volcanic outcrop in the distance. On the land side, thick green jungle bordered the sand.

I peered behind me, struck by the similarity of an outcrop guarding the beach in the other direction. I glanced back and forth, comparing. They were identical.

Is this another test? I wondered. With a momentary surge of hope, the thought occurred to me that maybe now I would actually have a chance to *do* something.

But what?

And if this were a test . . . did I really want to pass?

If I failed, I reasoned, perhaps I'd be rejected, saving mankind considerable grief and probably doing the aliens a favor as well. If they expected humans to be well-mannered domestics, they were in for a big surprise. I've eaten in enough greasy spoons throughout the galaxy to know that our race isn't much when it comes to service.

On the other hand, I thought, *maybe I'm supposed to fail.*

After more of this, I realized I was getting nowhere. With a shrug, I struck off down the beach. I hadn't gone more than a quarter mile when I heard something rustling in the jungle. Something big.

It was paralleling my course, snapping branches in the dark green undergrowth as it followed me. I picked up my pace, trying not to run. A minute later I stopped again to listen. Now I could make out the sound of its breathing—thick, heavy, guttural.

Sweat trickled down my forehead, stinging my eyes. As I watched, a thick stand of plants parted before me. Slowly, a snarl rumbling deep in its throat, a Vassorian tiger padded out onto the sand.

Vassorian tigers have long been extinct on their home world, but I once saw one in captivity. It weighed over two thousand kilos and could devour a man in seconds, with room left over for dessert. This one was even bigger. Never taking my eyes from the huge cat, I backed into the ocean. It crept forward, its platter-sized ears focusing on me like twin antennas. When I reached knee-deep water, I saw the tiger's hindquarters lower with a slight rocking motion. It was about to charge.

I turned and ran.

I got in two good strides before the sandy bottom fell off into deeper water. Behind me I heard the cat crashing through the shallows. I took a deep breath and dived. A talon caught my calf as I went under. I kicked for all I was worth, feeling a stab of pain as flesh ripped from my leg.

Somehow I got away.

I swam underwater for as long as I could. When I finally burst gasping to the surface, the tiger had returned to shore. It sat quietly, watching me tread water. Although its cold yellow eyes studied me impassively, I could tell from the twitching of its tail that it was angry. After a while it retreated into the jungle.

I stayed in the water for the rest of the day, berating myself for all the things I should have done that morning at first light. Instead of remaining exposed on the beach, I *should* have slipped into the jungle and searched for a place to hide. I *should* have found a weapon of some sort, too. I should have done a lot of things. But I didn't.

Now what?

Later that afternoon a school of tiny fish discovered me and proceeded to nibble at the ragged flesh of my calf. I had my hands full keeping them off. Although I worried that my blood might attract something larger, staying in the ocean seemed preferable to facing the tiger.

By the time the sun went down I was blue and shivering. Warily, I made my way ashore. No sign of the cat. I stood at the water's edge and listened.

Nothing.

The wind came up. I felt cold and exposed, and I didn't relish the idea of spending another night on the beach. With feelings of misgiving, I crept toward the jungle, deciding my best course lay in finding a suitable tree whose branches might provide a haven from the dangers lurking in the dark. I had almost made it to the jungle's edge when I heard a low growl behind me.

Mindless terror gripped me. I turned. The tiger crouched between me and the water.

My prior escape cut off, I ran for the trees.

This time the tiger came in quickly. It caught me before I'd gone a dozen steps. Squirming beneath it, I tried to fend it off with my hands, its fur coarse and wiry beneath my fingers, its breath hot and fetid on my face.

It was too strong.

Talons raked my chest, tearing slabs of flesh from my ribs. Snarling, the tiger took my head in its jaws. Slowly, inexorably, my skull splitting like a melon between those merciless gleaming teeth, I felt my life slip away.

This concludes the final exam.

I sat up. I was back on the deck of the alien ship, somehow still alive and in one piece. It had all been an illusion. "How . . . how did you do that?" I stammered.

The (unintelligible) creates sensory input based on primal fears in your subconscious.

"But it was so *real*."

Accurate testing requires accurate input.

"How does it work?" I asked, putting off what I knew I had to do next.

Surprisingly, they told me. It took less than a second. They just dumped it into my brain in one huge chunk. Even now I'm not sure why they did it. Maybe it was their idea of a joke, like when your kid asks how the holovid works and to get him off your back you tell him that frequency-modulated coherent light from solid-state emitters are phase-conjugated into three-dimensional standing waves, thus creating full-color visual images. Understand? No? Well, go ask your mother.

Anyway, they told me. It was too much for me to grasp then, but it came in handy later, not to mention extremely profitable. As I said, I have a good memory, and Axel can make just about anything work. But that's another story.

"I want another test," I said, fighting a splitting headache that had resulted from the aliens' data-dump into my cranium.

A long pause.

WHY?

"Why? You want to know why?" I shot back. "I'll tell you why. None of your damn business, that's why. Just give me another test!"

To be truthful, I didn't know why myself. I just wanted to do it again. As I said earlier, I'm as stubborn as they come, but anger was a big factor as well. They had kidnapped me, subjected me to degrading tests, even killed me inside their slimy slug thing, whatever they called it. But there was more to it than that. I didn't want to quit, not with the way things were. It had nothing to do with saving humanity. For all I knew, I was making things worse. I didn't care. I was mad. I couldn't give up. I *wouldn't*.

At last they answered.

Your request is granted.

Along with their response, I detected something else. *Anger? Disappointment?* I couldn't tell. Whatever their reasons, they gave me another test. And another.

And another.

I died many deaths. I was eaten by Thallasian spiders, flayed by Dogral whip-beetles, suffocated in Polaran quicksand. I lost a game of Russian roulette with an android. I even stopped a fusion meltdown on a jump-freighter, but got fried anyway when the radiation shields malfunctioned. I always lost, but every time I came out demanding the same thing. "I want another test!"

Eventually they refused.

"No way," I insisted. "Give me another test!"

Further testing will serve no purpose. You have failed.

"What?"

The purpose of the (unintelligible) is to determine whether a species can grasp the futility of resistance. From your testing, we conclude that humans lack the intelligence necessary to accept domination.

"Is that so? Well, let me tell you something, assho—"

This exchange is terminated.

". . . running through all our files, and I can't do anything about it." Axle peered at me expectantly. "What now?"

At first I was too shocked to speak. I glanced around the bridge. Everything looked the same. I mean exactly the same. According the ship's chronometer, absolutely no time had passed while I'd been gone. "Have I been missing for several watch cycles?" I asked shakily.

"Several watches? Quit kidding around, Cap. This is serious. What do you want to do?"

I shrugged. "Keep recording, I guess."

"Right. Hey, they're leaving!"

We stared in silence as the alien ship abruptly flickered to an orbit just above the accretion disc. Then it squeezed back into the black hole, apparently reversing the process by which it had come out.

"I don't believe it," said Axle, scratching his head in amazement as the glittering vessel disappeared.

"Yeah," I said. "And you don't know the half of it yet."

What Goes Up . . .

S uccess at last!

Flushed with excitement, George Simpson leaned over his workbench, eager to repeat the experiment. Nervously, he inserted another roller skate into copper coils, fighting to calm himself. The first time *couldn't* have been a fluke. He had seen it with his own two eyes!

Quickly, George readied his invention for another attempt. He worked meticulously, his eyes on the task before him, his mind on the money. What difference does it make if I don't understand how it works? he told himself. The important thing is that it will make money. A *lot* of money . . . assuming he could do it again.

"George?" his wife called down from the kitchen above. George glanced guiltily around the converted garage that served as his workshop, then continued working without answering.

"George!" his wife yelled again.

"Yes, Martha. What is it?" George finally responded, unable to mask the impatience in his voice.

"Don't you take that tone with me, George. Dinner is nearly ready. Finish whatever you're doing and come up."

"Be there soon," George lied.

Although George realized that Martha resented the hours he spent (wasted, as she put it) in his workshop, he also knew she had some justification for her attitude. Until now, excepting a considerable depletion of their savings, he hadn't accomplished anything with his experiments—a fact she invariably mentioned every time they discussed money. Scowling, George thought back to the numerous occasions she had pointed out that important scientific discoveries weren't made by someone like him working alone in a garage filled with scavenged electronic odds and ends.

Well, was she in for a surprise!

Carefully, George completed his preparations, regretting that he hadn't kept better records during his previous trials. When everything lay in readiness, the controls set as close as he could remember to the previous trial, he mentally crossed his fingers and tripped the power switch.

The lights in the room dimmed as current surged through his device. A low hum emanated from the workbench, slowly increasing to a throaty growl. George stared at the roller skate.

At first nothing happened. Abruptly, the skate lurched. Then, slowly, it levitated to the center of the copper coils. George felt sweat gathering under his arms, a thrill of anticipation building in the pit of his stomach. His eyes widened as a blue halo gradually surrounded the skate, sparks snapping from its rusty surface to the encircling copper coils. An instant later the skate began to shimmer, flecks of greenish iridescence playing across its surface.

This is it, George thought, barely able to contain his excitement.

The acrid smell of ozone became overpowering. George held his breath. The skate began to vibrate—turning translucent, ghostlike, insubstantial. Then, with a dazzling flash of light . . . it disappeared!

Exhilarated, George peered into the coils. Not a trace of the skate remained. It had vanished completely, just as the first skate had minutes earlier.

After turning off the power, George crossed the garage and sat at a small table near the stairs. He leaned back and propped his feet on the table's wooden surface. It works! he thought with a satisfied grin. It really works! Now, what am I going to do with it?

One by one, George considered possible applications for his invention, soon arriving at the most obvious—trash disposal. Throwaway items were everywhere, and once used, people needed a place to throw them away. Perhaps he had solved the world's garbage problem. The ultimate trash disposer—one in every home.

There *was* a catch, George realized uneasily. Where was the stuff going? It couldn't simply cease to exist. It had to be reappearing somewhere, and that could pose a problem. It certainly wouldn't do to have tons of garbage—or worse yet, spent nuclear fuel and so forth—reappearing in someone's backyard.

Hold on, George thought. What if he could get the objects that disappeared in his coils to reemerge someplace else— someplace *predictable*. Then he would really have something!

George knew what he had to do: more experiments! Whistling happily, he began looking around the garage for something else to place in his device.

*   *   *

In a region of the galaxy so distant from Earth that conventional measurement lost all meaning, the alien craft hung in the darkness of space.

Though unarmed, the *Polem*, or Treaty Verification Reconship FS1142 as she was formally titled, resembled most of the Federation's larger warships—a revolving G-ring with three axis arms connecting the command module to the drive cylinder, with two jump-nacelles mounted a safe distance from the crews' quarters. Fast and agile and crammed with the most sophisticated sensing devices available, she was designed for one single duty: reconnaissance.

Lieutenant Zorial sat at his console in the forward observation post, staring with horror into the viewing holocube. He couldn't believe his eye. Nevertheless, there it was, the ominous red tendrils of the Sigma explosion expanding in the holodisplay.

Zorial's mind recoiled from the consequences—a thousand years of peace with the Santori shattered in an instant! To make matters worse, the violation had happened on *his* watch, in *his* sector. With a looming sense of dread, he adjusted the viewfield, his tentacles moving rapidly over the control pegs. The explosion expanded, filling the entire cube. Zorial leaned closer.

The telltale signature of a Sigma detonation lay centered in the holocube, deadly and unmistakable, a Treaty violation of the greatest magnitude. Damn the Santori, Zorial thought angrily.

They know that retaliation on our part is mandatory. What are they trying to do, destroy us all?

Numb with shock, Zorial moved to the communications panel. But after actuating the subspace transmitter, he hesitated. Why would the Santori jeopardize a peace that has existed for a millennium? he wondered. The energy released by the unauthorized detonation had been minimal—probably not even enough to nova a single star—and it had taken place in an uninhabited sector.

Could there be some mistake? he wondered. Perhaps calling Lexxa was in order. Postponing the transmission, Zorial opened a channel to the crews' quarters. "Captain Lexxa?"

"What?" Lexxa's voice came back, thick with sleep.

"You need to get up here. Something's happened."

A slight hesitation. Then, "I'm on my way. But I warn you, Zor, you'd better have a damn good reason for waking me."

As he awaited the arrival of the *Polem's* other crew member, Zorial referred to the code book and began punching in the transmission ciphers. He had just finished entering the notification protocol when he heard the metal deck outside resounding with Lexxa's heavy tread. As he watched his captain enter, Zorial realized from the angle of her distended palps and the color of her abdominal segment that she wasn't in a good mood. Not even close.

"By the gods, what's so important that you have to—" Lexxa's words died on her mandibles as she spotted the glow in the holocube. "Great Maker," she hissed. "They finally did it."

"I've entered the notification codes," Zorial informed her. "They're ready to send."

"What are you waiting for? Do it immediately," Lexxa ordered, glaring her disapproval.

Quickly, Zorial sent the scrambled message, alerting Federation headquarters of the violation. Upon finishing, he realized that a technical state of war now existed with the Santori. With a hollow feeling, he stepped back from the communications console. Lexxa was still staring into the holocube, absorbed in the display. Guiltily, Zorial noticed she hadn't taken time to dress before coming to the observation deck. She had on only boots, sidearm, and the short sleeping-tunic she'd worn to bed. The satiny garment clung to her clean, strong limbs, barely covering the smoothness of her thoracic segment and the seductively dark chitin of her spiracle. Zorial looked away, thinking, not for the first time, that under different circumstances he and Lexxa might have been more than fellow officers. "Captain Lexxa?" he said, forcing his mind back to the problem at hand. "Something about this is bothering me."

"Bothering you?" Lexxa snarled. "You're a master of understatement, Zor. Our race is about to embark on the bloodiest conflict in recorded history, and instead of joining the glorious battle, we're stuck here on a reconship. Your being male, I don't expect you to understand, but it's more than 'bothering' me. If I were stationed on my regular ship assignment in the fleet right now, I could be targeting a retrocharge right down their slimy throats, or whatever you call that organ they eat with."

"Gastropore. But that's not what I mean, Captain. The Federation has maintained peace with the Santori for over fifty spawnings, right?"

"Correct. Mainly because our enemies know that if they challenge us, we'll nova their rotten planets straight to hell without a moment's hesitation."

"True. But we're not the only ones with Sigma weapons," Zorial countered. "The Santori have them, too. Neither of us has ever dared use them for fear of reprisal, so why would—"

"What's your point?"

Zorial lifted his antennae in a gesture of puzzlement. "Just this. A Treaty violation after all this time doesn't make sense."

"I disagree. You know the Santori."

"Granted, they're aggressive, but why would they risk war for the sake of a single Sigma test, or whatever it is we're seeing out there? They must have known we would detect it. If they wanted a fight, why didn't they just hit us with everything they've got?"

"I don't know," Lexxa said slowly. "But the unauthorized detonation out there is real. Our policy leaves no alternative but retaliation, and if that means war, so be it."

Zorial realized that Lexxa was right. The unthinkable was about to happen, with the weapons of destruction each race had held in readiness for generations finally used in an ultimate act of mutual genocide.

"Great Maker, not again!" Lexxa exclaimed, staring once more into the cube.

Zorial joined her. Together they watched as yet another Sigma explosion blossomed in the display, merging with the first.

"We should never have trusted them," Lexxa growled, brushing past Zorial and seating herself at the transmitter. "I'll notify headquarters of the second violation. I'm also recommending that we retaliate without delay."

"No!" Zorial choked, horrified by Lexxa's words. Although the *Polem* carried no armament, she *could* relay a Sigma retrocharge from one of the armed ships in the fleet. Once redirected, the retro would follow the violations' paths back through nullspace, detonating at their source. It was feasible . . . but it meant war, with no possibility of turning back.

"No?" hissed Lexxa, her eye blazing with fury. "Are you afraid to fight?"

"That's not it. I . . . I just think firing a retro weapon doesn't leave any room to negotiate. There may be—"

"Negotiate? I think not. Besides, the decision isn't ours. It will come from headquarters. And *whatever* their decision, Lieutenant Zorial, you will do your duty. Is that understood?"

"Yes, ma'am," Zorial replied. "Understood."

Zorial stood beside Lexxa as she completed her transmission. Afterward they waited in silence for a reply, knowing it would come soon. They were running out of time. The nullspace trails left by the violations would quickly disperse, and if they were to retaliate, it would have to be within the next few minutes. Zorial knew as well that if a retrocharge *were* sent, his cooperation would be essential. A Sigma relay was far too complex a task for one person to complete alone.

Can I do it? Zorial wondered numbly. Can I play a part in an action that will result in the death of billions?

Suddenly the radio crackled to life. Seconds later a decoded message flashed up on the screen.

TO: RECONSHIP POLEM FS1142 SECTOR A23L
FROM: FEDCENTCOM
PRIORITY TEXT:

TWO SIGMA-CLASS VIOLATIONS CONFIRMED. CONCLUDE SANTORI TESTING NEW WEAPON, POSSIBLE FIRST-STRIKE POTENTIAL. POLEM TO RELAY SIGMA RETRO FROM BATTLESHIP TICOR. CHARGE ARRIVAL IN EIGHT MINUTES.

END TRANSMISSION.

"Now that's more like it," Lexxa said coldly, keying the receipt code. "Open a wormhole to the *Ticor*. I'll get the relay system operational."

"Wait, Lexxa. What if—"

"Do it. There's no time for questions. If we're not prepared when the retrocharge comes through, we're dead."

Zorial knew that if they didn't relay the Sigma retrocharge when it exited the wormhole, it would detonate at its last point of entry, obliterating everything in their sector of space—including them. He hesitated. After a long pause, he came to a decision. Squaring his carapace, he stepped to the communications console and keyed the transmitter. "*Ticor*, this is Lieutenant Zorial, second officer of the *Polem*," he said, not bothering to scramble the message. "I refuse to assist in relaying the retrocharge."

"You coward!" Lexxa shouted, grabbing a tentacle and spinning him around.

Zorial found himself staring into the snout of Lexxa's service sidearm. His stomach twisted as he noticed that the weapon's power setting was locked on kill.

"Prepare for the Sigma relay," Lexxa warned. "Do it, Zor, or I swear I'll fry you right where you stand."

Nervously, Zorial eyed the blaster. "Captain, we can't go through with this," he said quietly. The consequences are unthinkable. Even if you shoot me, you still won't be able to complete the relay. There has to be another way."

Before Lexxa could reply, a voice crackled from the transmitter. *"Polem,* this is *Ticor.* We're firing shortly. Be ready."

Without lowering her weapon, Lexxa grabbed the microphone. *"Ticor,* we have a problem. My second officer refuses to assist with the relay. Please advise."

Zorial stood motionless. Lexxa still had her weapon trained on him, and he knew one wrong move meant death.

I'm dead anyway, Zorial thought morosely. If the Ticor didn't fire the retrocharge because of him, he would be court-martialed and executed. And if the retro was sent . . . they were all dead.

All at once the proximity alarm went off, its clanging signaling the approach of another vessel. Zorial and Lexxa turned to the viewscreen, staring in disbelief as a Santorian warbird flickered out of nullspace beside them, its mushroom-shaped hull dwarfing the *Polem.*

Lexxa adjusted the transmitter and spoke into the mike. "Santorian vessel, identify yourself."

"Federation ship, this is Captain Xi of the Santorian Alliance," came the reply, the voice from the translator circuits sounding flat and metallic. Zorial made an adjustment to the communications equipment, noting Lexxa's nod of approval as he patched her conversation with the alien intruder through to the *Ticor.*

"You are ordered to surrender your vessel," the Santorian continued. "You have one minute to comply."

"This is outrageous!" Lexxa spat back. "You break the Treaty, then threaten an unarmed Federation ship. Surrender? Never!"

"There *is* an alternative," the Santorian noted dryly. "If you fail to comply, I have been authorized to destroy you."

On impulse, Zorial spoke up. "Captain Xi, I assume from your presence that you intercepted our recent transmissions to the *Ticor*."

"Ah, Lieutenant Zorial. Yes, we've been listening to your communications with great interest. How convenient that you failed to transmit your last message in code. A bit *too* convenient, eh? If you think we can be so easily misled, you're mistaken. Of course you refused to relay the retrocharge. You would be sending it to destroy your own base. We know who's responsible for the Treaty violations: the Federation!"

"The Federation? But why? What would we have to gain?" asked Zorial, suddenly seeing a glimmer of hope.

The Santorian remained silent.

"I don't know what happened," Zorial pushed on rapidly, "but I *do* know that any further aggression by either of us will touch off a conflict that neither of our races will survive. Since your arrival, we've maintained a communication link with the *Ticor*. They're listening now. A hostile move by you will force them to retaliate. We may die first, but you'll be close behind— followed by billions on both our worlds. Don't let that happen, Captain."

A brief silence. Then, " I must confer with my superiors. If you attempt to leave, you will be destroyed."

The transmission abruptly ended. Zorial glanced at Lexxa. She was working at the communications console, her long, flexible digits snaking over the controls. She stopped and glared at Zorial. "They've cut our link with the Ticor," she snarled, her rage barely contained. Then, still glaring, "You're wasting your time with them. The Santori will never back down."

"It can't end like this," Zorial said softly. "If there's hope, we have to try."

Minutes later Captain Xi reestablished contact. "We seem to be at an impasse," he said. "Both our races deny responsibility for the Sigma violations. But there they are before us."

"At least we concur on something," Lexxa muttered. "What now?"

"What do *you* propose?"

Again Zorial spoke up. "Although unlikely, perhaps the explosions are the work of someone other than ourselves. If that is the case, why don't we determine who *is* responsible and then proceed from there?"

"Agreed. And I assure you that *whoever* it is, Federation or otherwise, they shall pay dearly for their recklessness," replied the Santorian. "How do we find them?"

"The *Polem* has the necessary sensors to trace the violations back to their source," Lexxa answered. "It is possible for you to join us," she added reluctantly, "but we'll have to leave without delay."

"Contact your superiors, Captain. I'll reconfer with mine."

Moments later, both sides having acceded to a temporary truce, the two vessels flickered in the darkness . . . and were gone.

*   *   *

Now here's something I'll never miss, George thought, lifting a bowling ball he had spotted on a shelf near the furnace. He hadn't bowled in years—not since throwing out his back working in the garden. It was perfect.

"George, dinner's getting cold," Martha called down insistently.

Burning with curiosity, George placed the ball into the coils. "Be right there," he yelled back.

"George, come up *now*."

"Gimme a couple more minutes, hon."

"It's ready now!"

"Oh, all right." Grumbling, George turned off the power to his apparatus.

I'll get up early and begin again first thing tomorrow morning, he promised himself, starting up the stairs. Maybe he would even be able to find out where the stuff was going. If not—well, then after the bowling ball he would try something even bigger.

George stopped on the top landing, taking one last look back at the tangle of wires and circuits and coils on his workbench, bowling ball ready within. His mood lifting at the sight, he flipped off the light, sending the room into darkness.

Tomorrow, he thought cheerfully as he headed into the kitchen. Tomorrow is going to be one hell of a day!

The Sacrifice

With a mix of confusion, and anger, and ineffable, bottomless despair, she realized that her Triad was about to die.

They had completed many missions together, but this time something had gone horribly wrong. She had sensed danger from the very beginning. Little things—an unwarranted tightening of security in Central Command, an inexplicable tension in the encoding technicians, a puzzling secrecy surrounding the message that had been embedded within her . . .

Shortly after departure, two Dark Ones had picked up their trace in a region normally devoid of enemy. When her calls for help had gone unanswered, her Triad had taken evasive action.

They had been unable to shake their pursuers.

In a final act of desperation, the two other members of her Triad—the double progeny from her only budding—had separated and turned back in an effort to delay the inevitable.

Moments later their death screams had echoed in her mind.

Now, terrified and alone, she fled through the hierarchies of space and time. In panic she entered a labyrinth of forbidden realities, twisting, turning . . . yet still they came.

Jake Sheridan felt lousy.

His back ached, his head throbbed, and he hadn't slept in thirty-six hours. Making things worse, over the past two days his life had unraveled in ways he would never have expected, and no matter what else happened, he was certain his mood couldn't sink any lower.

He was wrong.

Toying with his drink, Jake sat in a slowly revolving bar atop the ninety-second floor of the Ecstasy Pleasure Palace in West Los Angeles, glumly regarding the lights of the city below. With a sigh, he tossed down the dregs of his whiskey and decided to have another.

Jake hadn't felt like coming to the pleasure palace. That had been his friend Cameron's idea. Once there, Jake hadn't felt like getting drunk, either—although he realized he had already made serious progress in that department. But most of all, despite Cameron's solicitous counsel, he most certainly didn't feel like having sex with a cyborg.

"Jake? Over here, buddy. Punch line's coming up."

"Huh? Oh, sorry, Cam." Making an effort to shake his depression, Jake returned his attention to his friend across the table.

Cameron was a big man, nearly as big as Jake. As usual, Cameron was enjoying his own joke to a degree not warranted by the material. "First things first," Cameron said, noticing Jake's empty glass and ordering another round of cocktails on the drinkpad—whiskey-flavored synthol for Jake, beer for himself. "Now, where was I? Oh, yeah. So the last couple stands up in front of the congregation. 'Well,' says the minister. Have you kept—" Cameron paused, scowling as a hovercraft settled noisily onto the rooftop landing pad outside.

As Cameron waited for the rotor noise to abate, Jake let his eyes wander the Pleasure Palace bar, idly considering his friend's determined assertion that a tumble with a sex surrogate was just the thing to help him forget his post-breakup blues. Somehow, Jake doubted it. He wasn't prudish, nor was he prejudiced against cyborgs, as were many of his contemporaries. He simply didn't feel comfortable around them. There was something about cyborgs that didn't seem quite . . . right.

"Okay, one more time," Cameron continued when the air taxi finally departed. "So the final couple gets up. 'Have you kept your promise?' the preacher demands. 'Did you forego sex for a month, proving your love of God and your worthiness to join our congregation?'

"The guy and his wife look at each other. 'Well, to tell you the truth, Reverend,' the guy says, 'we did pretty good for the first two weeks, just like them other couples. But halfway into the third week my wife dropped a can of peas, and when she bent to pick it up, the sight of her got me all worked up. And, well . . . we wound up doin' it right there on the floor.'"

Cameron grinned, took a long pull on his beer, and belched. "So the preacher points to the door and says, 'You have proved yourselves unworthy and are no longer welcome in our congregation.' The guy shakes his head. 'I'm not surprised,' he says. 'They won't let us back in the supermarket, either.'"

By then their fresh drinks had arrived. Jake grabbed his whiskey, took a sip, and forced a smile, trying to show some appreciation for Cameron's effort to cheer him up. He and Cameron had been friends as long as he could remember. They had grown up in the same building complex, gone to the same schools, done their UN service together, even occasionally dated the same girls. They had shared everything . . . everything except Megan. Pulling his thoughts back from that dangerous territory, Jake bolted the rest of his drink and punched up another, glancing questioningly at Cameron.

Cameron shook his head, nursing his beer. "Better take it easy on the synthol if you want to get some action in here tonight," he advised, finally recovering enough from his own joke to speak.

"That was your plan, Cam, not mine."

"And a good plan it is. Just what the doctor ordered."

Irritably, Jake looked out the bar's floor-to-ceiling windows, regarding the city's highways and buildings and power grids that stretched as far as the eye could see. "Look at it out there," he said, changing the subject. "Have you ever really *looked* at it?"

"Our fair city? Sure. What about it?"

"Nothing. Just that from up here you can see it for what it really is—a living, breathing organism that has covered nearly every square inch of our planet, spreading everywhere like a malignant growth."

"Malignant growth? Jeez, lighten up, pal." Cameron regarded his friend for a long moment, then sighed. "Don't take this wrong, Jake, but I never liked Tiffany. Nobody did. You're better off without her."

"Drop it."

"But it's not just her, is it? It's having to give up your berth on the colony ship."

Jake glared. "Yeah, that's definitely part of it," he admitted angrily. "Do you blame me? Emigrating to Regula-4 was my chance at a new life. Our chance at a new life. You and Megan, me and . . ."

". . . the bitch Tiffany?"

Jake nodded. "She had to know I couldn't find another partner in time, especially not with the colony pregnancy requirement."

"Of course she knew. She didn't care. Face it, Jake. She never planned to become an indentured colonist. She used you to get what she wanted, and then dumped you. End of story. I hear she moved into a plush Westside penthouse with some fat rich guy." Cameron hesitated. "She's not pregnant anymore, either."

Jake looked away. "Yeah. I heard that, too."

Both men fell silent as Jake's fresh drink arrived. After their waitress departed, Jake raised his glass. "I'm going to miss you, Cam. You and Megan. More than I can say."

Cameron somberly touched his glass to Jake's. "Same here, pal."

Another hovercraft landed outside, disgorged its passengers, and lifted off. "You'll get another planet," Cameron continued when the noise had again diminished.

"Maybe. But planets like Regula-4 don't come along that often—G-type sun, Earth-friendly environment, no dominant intelligent species."

Cameron finished his beer. "Are you going to see us off in the morning?"

"Yeah."

"Megan wants your promise that you'll be there."

"I'll be there. I haven't notified the Company that we're . . . that I'm not going. I'll let them know first thing tomorrow. Probably make some alternate pair's day. I just wish . . . ah, the hell with it."

"Right. At this point, there's nothing you can do but get on with your life. And take it from me, Jake, a little sugar will go a long way toward getting you over the hump, no pun intended."

"Cam—"

"C'mon, Jake," Cameron insisted, punching up the sex-surrogate catalog on the tabletop screen. "At least take a look."

"You look."

"Fine. I will," said Cameron, beginning to scroll through the cyborgs displayed in the table's translucent surface.

As Cameron perused the sex-surrogate selections, Jake once more glanced around the room. Across the crowded dance floor he noticed a female cyborg ascending a ladder that accessed a small balcony above the bar. Once there she began swaying to the background music, her nude body seductively shrouded in a holographic mist that rose and fell in colorful wisps, first concealing, then revealing—a flash of leg, the arch of her back, the smoothness of her breasts. Except for the slender steel control collar encircling her neck and the absolute, unfaltering perfection of her movements, Jake realized with a start that he might have mistaken her for human. Tearing away his eyes, he concentrated on his drink.

"Hey, check out this one!" said Cameron, tapping the tabletop screen. "The Terry Series. Red hair, blue eyes, and legs that won't quit."

"No redheads."

"Oh, right, I forgot. Tiffany has forever ruined you for redheads, you poor bastard. Okay, *you* pick."

"No, thanks."

"That's the spirit." Shaking his head sadly, Cameron continued his search.

Ignoring his friend, Jake stared into the watery remnants of his drink, dejectedly mulling over the turn of events that had derailed his chance to leave Earth—at least for the moment. In that regard, he knew Cameron was right. He would get another chance. It might take years, but sooner or later the Company would open up another planet, and with Jake's qualifications—degrees in both hydroponics and animal husbandry, a more than passing knowledge of mining, and the fact that he had already completed the Company's fourteen-month colonization training—he knew he stood an excellent shot of being selected again the next time around, assuming he could find a willing partner.

So why am I so depressed? Jake wondered. Is it losing Cam and Megan? Or is it that Tiffany had someone in the wings all along, and I was the last to know? Or is it that she terminated her pregnancy without even telling me?

"Here we go," said Cameron, again tapping the screen. "The Lara Series. Just released. Tall, beautiful, and not one red hair anywhere on their gorgeous nubile bodies."

"Sorry, Cam," said Jake, shaking his head as he saw his friend pushing a button to summon a hostess. "I appreciate the offer. I really do. I know you're trying to help, but I'm going home and sleep it off."

"'Scuse me a sec," said Cameron, spotting a surrogate hostess approaching. "Don't go anywhere."

Ignoring Jake's protests, Cameron rose and conferred with the surrogate hostess, then returned. "Trust me on this one, pal," he said. "Just follow the hostess over there. The fee is already paid, and this is *exactly* what you need. And Jake? Try to loosen up a little. It's only a cyborg."

She couldn't allow herself to be captured, for to do so would allow the information she carried to fall into enemy hands. She also knew she couldn't outrun them. There was only one hope for escape—to conceal herself and wait for help. Using the precious seconds earned by the deaths of her offspring, she coiled her fields and entered a nearby bubble of space-time. Somehow, she had to survive.

With a dazzling burst of light, she materialized among the stars. The Dark Ones would not be far behind. In her present form she would stand out like a beacon. Fighting panic, she searched for a place to hide.

A myriad of galaxies filled the four-dimensional bubble she had chosen, each galaxy containing billions of stars. In the nearest of these stellar swirls she began her search. Her race had long known that rudimentary life existed in these lower dimensions—usually primitive molecular assemblies of nuclear ash from nova stars. Her plan was to cloak herself in one of these organic forms. A degrading prospect, but preferable to capture and death.

Now it was her only hope.

Jake stood in the hallway, watching as the surrogate hostess departed. He hesitated, trying to decide what to do next. A card slot and a single raised panel broke the otherwise featureless surface of the door before him. He'd originally had no intention of going through, but curiosity was beginning to get the better of him. Besides, Cameron had already paid the fee, which was nonrefundable. Why not at least check things out?

Although suspecting he was making a mistake, Jake withdrew his wallet, inserted his ID card into the slot, and pushed the panel. The door swung smoothly inward. Again, he hesitated. Then, with a shrug, he entered. The door slid shut silently behind him, disappearing into the background.

Jake surveyed his surroundings, grudgingly admitting that the holographic illusion in which he found himself looked authentic down to the last detail, giving the impression that he had stepped from the plastic and steel of the twenty-second century into some long-extinct tropical paradise. Overhead the sky was gradually darkening to the deep purple of dusk; in the west a crescent moon hung low on the horizon.

Jake shook his head in amazement. Everything seemed so real—a soft touch of wind on his face, the musky smells of the rain forest, the clean white beach beneath his feet. Resisting the impulse to take off his shoes, he moved to a stand of palms bordering a small lagoon nearby. Upon arriving, he sensed movement to his right. He turned, peering into the glade.

As his eyes adjusted to the dimness, Jake could make out the outline of an elevated platform, supported between two towering mangroves. The structure appeared to have grown from the very forest itself—woven vines and roots composing its legs and frame, the latter supporting a bed of dried ferns and moss. And standing beside it was the most hauntingly beautiful woman Jake had ever encountered.

Eyes lowered, long auburn hair framing her lovely face and spilling over her bare shoulders, she made her way toward him. Her torso was lean and trim, her breasts high and full. As she neared, Jake realized with a tinge of surprise that she was nearly as tall as he.

A moment later she stood before him. She wore a small pair of gold earrings and a stainless-steel cyborg collar around her neck, nothing else. Jake found himself at loss for words. This wasn't what he had expected. She seemed almost . . . human. There was still the control collar to remind him she wasn't, of course. That, and something absent in her pale blue eyes—eyes that dilated slightly as she spoke. "Client: Sheridan, Jake. Service billing prepaid by Gilbert, Cameron E., credit card number 17634022714413220812."

"Nice to meet you, too," Jake grumbled, belatedly realizing that his sarcasm was undoubtedly wasted on a cyborg.

"What is your desire, and how may I assist you in fulfilling it?" the cyborg asked, her voice soothing and melodic.

"My desire? Actually, I'm not even sure what I'm doing here," Jake replied, not accustomed to speaking with a female whose eyes were nearly on a level with his—*especially* one showing as much bare skin as this one, even if she were a cyborg. "My buddy thinks . . ." Jake stopped, suddenly feeling foolish to be explaining himself. "What's your name?"

"Lara Series number eight-five-one, or simply Lara if you wish," the cyborg responded. "Do you have a particular fantasy in mind?" When Jake didn't reply, she continued. "Are these surroundings to your liking? I can change them if you want. It's possible to simulate a desert oasis, a luxury penthouse, a mountain cabin with a warm cozy fire—anything you want."

Jake ignored her offer. He'd had a lot to drink, but he wasn't *that* drunk. "Aren't you cold?" he asked, trying not to stare.

"Cold? Oh, I understand. You would like me in something less revealing." Lara touched her collar. An instant later a peach-colored negligee with high, V-shaped cuts up each side materialized on her body. The silky fabric clung to her seductively, doing little to conceal her figure. "Better?" she asked with a playful spin that caused the holographic garment to flare around her thighs.

Surprised to find himself attracted, Jake remained silent. He knew that the cyborg was no more real than the other surroundings in the holochamber, and that he would probably regret staying longer. Still, he made no move to leave.

"I sense your discomfort," said Lara. "It's a common reaction of humans unaccustomed to the presence of cyborgs. Perhaps you would feel more at ease if you knew something about me."

Again, Jake said nothing.

"Like you, I am composed of flesh and blood," she continued. "My body is fully operational; I eat, sleep, eliminate waste, and perform all the physiologic functions. Also like you, I am capable of experiencing both pleasure and pain. The main difference between us is that certain cognitive centers in my brain have been replaced with photonic circuitry—neural structures that are under the direct control of a central processor in this building. In addition, where you have a spleen, I have a self-contained energy source sufficient to power my bioelectric components for the remainder of my life. There are other changes, but they are insignificant."

Already aware of the differences between humans and cyborgs, Jake had listened to her with growing impatience, but toward the end something caught his attention. "What do you mean, for the rest of your life? You can die?" he asked.

"Of course. My body ages like yours, although at a considerably slower rate."

"How much slower?"

"I was cloned and brought to full physical maturity over a period of eighteen months. I am now three years old. Barring accident, I will remain physically unchanged for the next one hundred and ninety-seven years, after which my body will rapidly deteriorate."

"And then?"

"My photonic brain, which has a potentially indefinite lifespan, will be removed. If deemed appropriate, I will be given another body. If not, I will be deactivated."

"And that doesn't bother you?"

"No. Why should it?"

Surprised, Jake thought a moment, then laughed aloud, struck by the ludicrous situation in which he found himself. Here he was in a fantastic albeit illusory paradise with a willing, whiplash-gorgeous although equally illusory partner, and somehow he had managed to turn the conversation to thoughts of mortality.

Maybe Cam is right, he thought. Maybe I do need to loosen up. At any rate, I can't leave yet. If I return to the bar this early, I'll never hear the end of it from Cam. "Okay, Lara, or whatever your name is," he said. "Are you programmed to give a massage?"

"Anything you desire."

"Fine. That's what I want. And that's *all* I want. Just a massage."

Though still plagued by the suspicion he was making a mistake, Jake followed the cyborg to the arboreal bed, stripped to his shorts, and lay facedown on the soft, mossy surface. Despite his uneasiness, he felt his body quickly relaxing as her strong fingers, slippery with fragrant oil from a vial she withdrew from beneath the bed, began kneading the muscles of his shoulders and neck. Next her hands traveled his back and legs, maintaining a deep, steady rhythm. Jake closed his eyes, feeling himself drifting into a comfortable, if slightly inebriated, sleep.

"Turn over," Lara commanded twenty minutes later. "I'll do your hands and arms next."

Jake rolled onto his back. Lara knelt beside him on the bed, her long legs tucked neatly beneath her. Taking his left hand, she began working his fingers and knuckles, the web of his thumb, and the cords of his forearm.

A warm breeze drifted in, redolent with the sweetness of tropical blooms and the lush smells of the jungle. Jake looked up, noticing that the cyborg's auburn hair seemed to gleam as it fanned over her shoulders onto the fullness of her breasts.

"Does this feel good?" Lara asked without glancing up.

"Ummm," Jake murmured. Then, easing up on one elbow, "Listen, I'm curious about something you said earlier."

"Yes?"

"That bit about feeling pleasure and pain. When you make love, do you experience, uh . . ."

"Orgasm? Of course. As I said, I'm fully functional. Here, let me demonstrate." Before Jake could object, Lara swung a long, perfectly proportioned leg over his hips and straddled him.

"No, wait—"

"It's all right," said Lara, gently pushing Jake's shoulders back onto the bed. "It's not necessary for you to respond if you don't want to. I can do it all." Then taking his face in her hands, she kissed him. Jake could feel her breasts trailing lightly across his chest, her nipples hard and erect, and whatever he had been about to say was suddenly forgotten.

Slowly Lara began moving her hips in small circles, the warmth between her legs tantalizing, first pressing into him, then releasing. Taking her lips from his, she arched her back, exposing the long white curve of her neck and the thrust of her breasts. Gradually her flimsy nightgown turned from silky peach to fiery red, then became diaphanous, insubstantial, and finally disappeared altogether.

Still gently rocking, Lara lowered her head. Slippery from the massage, her hands explored Jake's shoulders, his arms, his chest. Her breath coming in increasingly ragged gasps, she intensified her tempo. And as she did, Jake felt himself responding. Reaching out, he ran his palms over the smoothness of her breasts. Gasping with pleasure at his touch, Lara closed her eyes. A sheen of perspiration glistened on her shoulders. A bead of moisture trickled down her chest, tracing a wet rivulet down her flawless skin. Abruptly, Jake felt her stiffen in a series of prolonged, delicious shudders, and a low sweet moan escaped her lips.

Running his fingers through her hair, Jake marveled at its softness. Again Lara brought her mouth to his, her lips softly insistent. He sensed his desire swelling, whatever reservations he'd had earlier dissipating like smoke in a windstorm. Lara shifted slightly. Still holding his lips with hers, she reached between her legs and gently guided him inside.

Jake closed his eyes. Waves of pleasure began building within, one upon another. There was no turning back, nor did he want to. Aware only of Lara, he abandoned himself to the ecstasy of her touch.

Beginning her search, she extended the tendrils of her consciousness into the nearest galaxy, randomly selecting a tiny star on the far reaches of one of the swirling arms. She chose well. The third planet circling the sun there teemed with life.

She had mere seconds before the Dark Ones arrived. She needed to find a suitable organism in which to hide.

An instant later she made her choice.

Jake's passion crested and flooded and burst inside her. Lost in the moment, he circled Lara with his arms. Inexplicably, instead of returning his embrace as she was surely programmed to do, she began struggling, surprising him with her strength.

Puzzled, Jake gazed into her eyes, recoiling from what he saw. Pain suddenly gripped him in a blinding fist of agony. A scream on his lips, Jake Sheridan descended a long dark tunnel into unconsciousness.

*   *   *

Darkness. And then . . . light!

She tasted her new world, astonished at the richness of sensation she was able to perceive. Although nearly overcome by its complexity, of one thing she was certain: A weapon of some kind was being thrust into her. She was being attacked!

Instinctively, she pushed with her mind. Hard. Her assailant screamed. She pushed again. With a shudder, her assailant fell silent.

Fighting to control her alarm, she inspected the organism that had been attacking her. How had it known? she wondered. Sensing it still lived, she decided to question it later. First she needed to examine the primitive data banks embedded in her new form.

Seconds passed as she assimilated the language, customs, and behavioral information contained in her body's rudimentary memory. When she had completed her inventory, she knew she had made a grave mistake.

Two mistakes, actually.

First, the beings of this world—humans, they called themselves—considered the form she had taken to be no more than a bionic machine, property to do with as they chose. Worse, she couldn't risk changing to another form. By now the Dark Ones had surely broached this dimension and would detect her if she did, even if the switch to a new body took only an instant.

Second, and more immediate—the cries of the organism she had subdued were certain to bring others. Lara glanced at the unconscious human, unsure of how to proceed. Before she could decide, a door slid open behind her. Rising from the bed, she watched as two additional humans entered. Quickly she touched their minds, questioning them without their knowledge—surprised that even creatures as primitive as they could exist without mind-to-mind contact.

The cyborg technician, as she now knew him to be, moved to the unconscious figure on the bed. The other hurried to a hidden alcove and threw a switch, turning off the room's holographic projectors. The illusion created by the machines abruptly vanished. Around them the tropical paradise reverted to a large rectangular room—translucent plastic walls, a simple bed, air-conditioning ducts traversing the ceiling, speakers and holoprojectors mounted high in all four corners. A moment later a bank of overhead lights came on, flooding the chamber with harsh white illumination.

The technician left the man on the bed and rejoined the other human. "What happened?" he demanded, staring at Lara.

She had to say something. "The organism attacked me and then lost consciousness," she replied, startled by the sound of her own voice.

"Not verbally!" the second human ordered, pointing to an opaque panel on the far wall. "Put it up on the screen."

As she searched her host memory for an appropriate response, Lara realized that the technician was regarding her a bit too closely. "Organism?" the man said. "Is that what you called him?"

When Lara didn't reply, the technician spoke to a concealed audio pickup in the ceiling. "Hal, this is Collins. Run a diagnostic on eight-five-one. We may have a malfunction. I'll help deactivate her from here."

Lara took a step backward.

"Hold still," the technician ordered.

Ignoring him, Lara continued to retreat. Suddenly she felt a tingling in the metal collar around her neck, along with the presence of a primitive electronic mind accessing her host memory. They were trying to turn off her body. She could not allow that. Grasping her collar, she shifted a layer of atoms in the slim metal casing. A section of the collar dissolved in her fingers. With a clatter, the glowing photonic circuits enclosed within spilled like jewels onto the floor.

The technician's eyes widened. "What the . . . ? Cyborgs can't function without a collar. How—"

The other human began pulling his friend toward the door. "Let's get out of here," he said nervously. "Let security handle this."

She had to act. As primitive as these humans were, they had somehow already discovered her presence. She didn't know how they knew, but things were about to get worse. Again she reached out with her mind. Quickly she subdued the flickers of consciousness in the two before her, careful not to extinguish them completely.

How fragile these beings are, she thought as they collapsed to the floor.

Then came another thought.

Others will come.

She could subdue them as well, but how long could she continue? It would take time for Command to locate her, and billions of humans inhabited the planet. Could she subdue them all? And even if she could, might not the resulting disturbance attract the Dark Ones?

Once again she realized she had miscalculated. Hiding among these organic creatures would prove more difficult than expected. If she were to survive, she couldn't afford another mistake. Rapidly she rifled through the minds of the humans on the floor, then the one on the bed. By the time she was finished, she had formed the outline of a plan.

Minutes later a tall woman wearing loosely fitting men's clothes entered a turbolift to the roof. She rode in silence, speaking to no one. Upon arriving at the taxi zone, she crossed to the landing pad, entered a waiting hovercab, and departed.

*   *   *

With a groan, Jake eased himself from the taxi, stepping onto the rooftop landing pad of his building complex. The throb between his temples was worse than ever, but with the exception of that, the pleasure-house medics had been unable to find anything wrong with him. They'd had no explanation for what had happened to him in the holochamber, either. In fact, they had become increasingly accusatory when *he* had been unable to supply an answer himself. The cops who had grilled him had been even less cordial.

"Take care, amigo," Cameron called from the interior of the cab, shouting to be heard over the rotor whine. "You're still seeing us off tomorrow, right?"

"I'll be there."

"Sorry about tonight."

"Not as sorry as I am," Jake yelled back. "Should have picked the redhead," he added wryly to himself as the hovercab rose into the night. Then, lowering his head against the rotor blast, he crossed to the rooftop elevator.

Perched nine hundred feet above the street, Jake's quarters occupied one of the more prestigious sections of the building complex in which he lived. Ignoring curious stares from other passengers who entered the lift along the way, Jake descended forty-seven levels to his apartment in silence—his feet bare, the ill-fitting clothes he had borrowed from the pleasure house stretched tight on his large frame. On the descent, not for the first time, he puzzled over the evening's events.

When he had regained consciousness, the cyborg was gone, along with his clothes. Like the other men there who were attacked, he couldn't remember much. The authorities had learned most of what happened from the security recordings. Jake had been able to add little. He had refrained from mentioning what he'd seen in the cyborg's eyes, deciding they wouldn't have believed him anyway.

When the elevator stopped at his floor, Jake exited, resolving to forget things for the moment. All he wanted to do now was sleep. Exhausted and still slightly drunk, he stumbled down the hallway to his quarters, punched his security code into the door panel, and entered. Once inside, he froze.

A light was burning in the entry. Jake was certain that he had turned off all lights before leaving earlier that evening. Moving quietly, he crept to the hall closet and grabbed a three-iron from his golf bag. Club in hand, he peered into the living room. A flicker from the holovid danced against the far wall.

What sort of thief turns on the HV?

An instant later he saw her standing in the darkness, studying her own three-dimensional image in the HV viewing cube. The cyborg! Jake tightened his grip on the iron and stepped into the room. "What . . . what are you doing here?" he demanded, noting that she had a news broadcast on the display. She also had on his clothes.

Ignoring him, the cyborg continued watching the late-night news, listening as a handsome news anchor described that night's incident at the Ecstasy Building. The newscaster concluded his piece by warning that authorities considered the escaped cyborg extremely dangerous. Then came a short addendum in which a spokesperson for BioRobotics Inc. insisted that Lara 851's programming made it impossible for her to harm a human. Nonetheless, the company's representative had no explanation for why the removal of her control collar had not rendered the sex surrogate inoperable—further stating that the entire Lara series was being recalled.

Next the HV display began flipping through channels, stopping briefly on other stations covering the "Rogue Cyborg" story. Puzzled, Jake glanced at the bookcase, spotting the HV remote control still sitting on the shelf.

The holocube abruptly flicked off. Jake tripped a light switch by the door. "What are you doing here? he repeated.

The cyborg turned toward him, her eyes arrogant and chilling. "I do not intend to harm you," she said. "Unless you make that necessary."

Tightening his grip on the golf club, Jake took a step backward, regretting his rash entrance.

"I thought you were attacking me," she continued. "The other humans tried to deactivate me. I had to stop them."

Jake shot a look at the front door, considering making a run for it. "How did you get in?"

Lara withdrew Jake's wallet from a jacket pocket and tossed it onto the coffee table. "I used your credit card to travel here to the address given on your identification."

"A credit card is no good without the personal code. And how did you enter my quarters?"

"I know your credit card code. I know your door code as well. I know everything about you, Jake Sheridan."

"How?"

"I accessed your memory."

"Sure you did." Jake shot another glance at the door. "What do you want?"

99

"Because of what happened tonight, the authorities are searching for me."

"You've got that right."

"In order to escape, I require assistance. You will provide it."

Jake shook his head. "Wrong. Why should I help you?"

The cyborg took a step closer. "Because I know what you most want, Jake Sheridan. I will give it to you in exchange for your help. If you refuse, I can force you to comply. Either way, you *will* assist me. Tomorrow we will leave this planet together aboard your colony transport vessel."

A chill ran up Jake's spine. "How do you know about the colony transport?"

"I told you. I know everything about you. *Everything.*"

Again, Jake shook his head. "I'll admit I want to get on that colony ship tomorrow more than anything, but there's no way I'm doing it with you. Besides, it would never work. All emigrating females must already have a child or be at least six weeks pregnant at the time of—"

"I know these things," the cyborg interrupted, moving closer. "You misunderstand me. Look."

Jake tried to back away. For some reason he found himself unable to move. His brain sent the message; his body simply didn't respond. Paralyzed, he watched as the cyborg approached.

Lara's eyes held him, drew him, seeming to grow larger, larger . . . at last becoming black, bottomless pools. Powerless to flee, Jake gazed into a void that suddenly sprang from her eyes, watching in wonder as it filled with stars, and then galaxies, and then universe upon universe. Bewildered, he traveled with her through a myriad of dimensions as she showed him the horror from which she fled. And then she showed him something else.

Jake stared, refusing to accept it. In a distant part of his mind he could hear her explaining how she had regenerated the sterilized tissues of her body, modified a cell, joined it to his seed, and caused it to grow at an accelerated rate. She showed him what she had created. And then she told him what he must do to have it.

Jake's mind reeled. Through her eyes, he could see it growing deep within her. Tiny, but already recognizable. A child.

His child.

* * *

Early the next morning, a throng of colonists departing for Regula-4 stood assembled on the colony transport embarkation platform. Lara followed Jake through the initial checkpoint. There she underwent a brief N-scope exam to confirm her pregnancy. Next she and Jake received a series of travel inoculations. Proceeding on, they signed contracts that bound them as indentured Company employees for the next seven years. Finally, emigration papers in hand, they made their way through the milling crowd to the shuttle loading bay. During this entire time Lara made certain to stay close to her human companion, watching him for any sign of betrayal.

"Jake! Over here."

Lara peered across the mass of humans, spotting a man and woman approaching from the far side of the loading platform. When they arrived, Jake glanced in her direction, then back at the two humans. "Megan, Cam, you, uh, know Tiffany, right?" he said.

The man called Cameron stared. "Huh?"

"Just play along," Jake whispered. "Please. I'll tell you about it on the transport."

Cameron narrowed his eyes at Lara but remained silent.

"Hi, gorgeous," Jake continued nervously, bending to kiss the slim blond woman who had accompanied Cameron across the room.

Megan returned Jake's kiss with a hesitant smile. Then she glanced at Lara. "What's going on, Jake? I know who she is. Her face was all over this morning's newscast. Despite that awful wig of Tiffany's she's wearing, others are sure to—"

"Not now," Jake interrupted.

"But . . ."

"Let it go, Megan. Please. I'll fill you in later."

"I hope you know what you're doing."

"I don't have much choice," said Jake. Then, in an effort to change the subject, he turned to a small boy whom Lara had missed earlier. The child was standing quietly behind Megan, regarding the other humans solemnly.

"Hey, who's this good-looking kid?" Jake asked, ruffling the child's hair.

"Hi, Jake," the boy said, his face breaking into a grin.

"Hi, Adam. Ready to go to your new home?"

"You bet!"

"We all are," said Cameron, still staring at Lara. "You know which shuttle you're on?"

"Not yet," Jake answered.

"You'd better check. I'll go with you."

Jake turned to Lara. "Stay here," he said. "I'll be right back. Please don't hurt anyone," he added softly.

As Jake and Cameron headed across the loading platform, Megan regarded Lara for a long moment. "What did he mean— don't hurt anyone?"

Lara remained silent.

When Lara didn't respond, Megan pushed on. "Nice outfit," she remarked dryly.

Finally Lara spoke. "Jake supplied these clothes from his closet. He said they belonged to a human female named Tiffany."

"I recognize them." Another long pause, then, "You're the cyborg that the authorities are searching for. Where's your collar? I thought cyborgs couldn't function without a collar. And how'd you get past the N-scope? Speaking of which, how did you even manage to get past the gate without a colony ID?"

Again Lara didn't respond, sensing something dangerous about the human named Megan.

"Why is Jake taking you with him?"

Briefly, Lara considered silencing the troublesome human. She rejected that course, deciding too many others were present. At any rate, the mental effort she was using to manipulate the one called Jake—not to mention deceiving the humans at the admission gate and at the N-scope station—was both tenuous and tiring. She concluded from Jake's demeanor that the safety of the woman, as well as that of her husband and child, might be a more effective way to control his actions.

"You're not going to answer?" Megan persisted. "Lara, or whoever you are, I hope you understand what Jake is sacrificing for you."

"He is sacrificing nothing. He wishes to leave this planet. So do I. We made a pact."

"A pact? We're leaving everything behind—home, family, friends. When we arrive at Regula-4, Cam and I will have each other, and Adam. What will Jake have? A pact with you? That's not enough."

Lara's thoughts returned unbidden to the lost members of her Triad, and she felt a terrible loneliness welling within. Unexpectedly, she understood what the human named Megan meant by her words.

"Nothing to say?" Megan continued angrily. "All right, then. I'll make this simple. I don't understand what's going on here, but Jake and I have been friends for a long time. If any harm comes to him because of you, I will make you regret it."

Lara sat beside Jake on the shuttle as it ascended a magnetic transit loop into low orbit. During the journey she felt the eyes of many upon her. Ignoring them, she rode in silence.

After matching velocity with the *Patriot*—the giant warship that would be the colonists' home for the upcoming weeks during transit—the shuttle docked and Lara disembarked with the others, grateful to feel the sensation of gravity again on the warship. Gradually, the nausea that had tormented her new body during the shuttle ride gradually began to abate. The organic shell in which she had cloaked herself seemed so sensitive at times, so frail. She wondered how this race of beings had survived as long as they had. Granted, their history wasn't that long, but still . . .

Shortly after boarding the *Patriot*, all colonists were placed in stasis. It was a routine procedure; even a ship the size of the colony transport could not provide food, water, and waste disposal for five hundred colonists during transit. Unlike the humans, although her body was inactivated like theirs, even in stasis Lara remained aware, and during the early days of the journey she spent a good deal of time puzzling over why she hadn't heard from Command. Although she had been unable to send a call for help, for doing so would disclose her position to the Dark Ones, those at headquarters must surely be aware of her absence.

Why hadn't they sent help?

As the days passed, Lara grew bored. Idly, she perused the ship's onboard computer. Eventually she absorbed the entire contents of its memory, including a vast library of fictional works and a diverse selection of technical publications covering subjects from physiology, anatomy, and molecular biology to mathematics, chemistry, medicine, and physics. And gradually, despite the humans' obvious limitations, she began to find a few of their aspects intriguing. Their music, for instance, was fascinating—far more than the sum of its parts. And who would have guessed that their social interactions, even without mind-to-mind contact, could be so complex?

To relieve her boredom, she also turned her mind inward and examined the growing spark that was developing in her womb. At first she had been content to simply monitor its development, but before long she began to take an active part—making small additions and subtle alterations to the minuscule clump of cells. It was an interesting diversion, but one she knew she couldn't continue much longer. Help would soon come, and she had made irreversible modifications to the physical form that she'd taken. When she departed, her body would perish—along with the child she had started within.

But slowly, as the insignificant bit of life unfolded and changed and grew inside her, Lara's new body began to change as well.

Twenty-two days after departure, ship's coordinate time, the *Patriot* dropped out of warpspace and emerged once more into the space-time continuum. Dead ahead the central star of the Regula system burned brightly, and six hours later the colony transport swung into orbit around the fourth planet out. Upon scanning the new world, the *Patriot's* sensors revealed that Regula-4 had undergone significant climatic changes since the Company's last survey. The planet's mean surface temperature had fallen nearly two degrees—not much in the geologic scheme of things, but enough to begin locking up water-ice in the polar caps. Snow now covered a large portion of the landmasses in both hemispheres.

The science team was unable to determine whether the meteorological development was a temporary cycle or a harbinger of something worse. Nevertheless, because the *Patriot* carried insufficient fuel to transport all five hundred emigrants back to Earth, most had no choice but to depart. Although it was possible for a few to return home, of the five hundred colonists who had made the journey, four hundred and ninety-one elected to stay.

A revised landing site was chosen closer to the equatorial plane, and two days later all forty-seven cargo shuttles, laden with passengers, supplies, and equipment, descended to the surface. Shortly afterward the *Patriot* lifted out of orbit, leaving the colonists to fend for themselves.

The first weeks on the wintry planet were devastating.

Each night the air turned colder; each day the winds grew stronger. Shelter and warmth being of primary concern, all energies were initially devoted to assembly of the null-field domes, leaving a huge mound of mining gear, farming equipment, and transportation vehicles to be reclaimed after the spring thaw . . . if it ever came.

A dome of sufficient size to house the entire community, at least temporarily, was quickly erected. Next, lesser domes were energized. By the time snow from the escalating storms covered the frozen ground, the core of the base had been constructed— central fusion reactor operational, hydroponic tanks and food processors online, medical facilities functional. At that point, although nine colonists had succumbed to the harsh environment, morale was high. The settlement's chief problem consisted of several puzzling cases of fever that had broken out in one of the perimeter domes. Concluding that Company physicians had missed an organism when they were developing their inoculation regime, the colony medical team quarantined all sick members and began searching for the fever's cause.

During these first days, having decided her best course lay in avoiding all unnecessary interaction with the humans, Lara requested separate quarters and spoke to no one, not even Jake. Except to eat, she remained in her cubicle in the main dome. As a result, more and more she was shunned.

It came to a head late one evening of the third week. Lara was sitting by herself in the nearly deserted cafeteria, eating a gruel of protein and carbohydrate—a product of the newly functioning hydroponic tanks. She found it delicious. Eating was one thing about her present situation that she had come to enjoy, and enjoy immensely. And curiously, no matter how much she ate, she always seemed to be hungry.

Nearing the end of her meal, she noticed Jake crossing the room toward her. She ignored him, concentrating on finishing her meal.

Jake sat across from her at the table. "Is this how you keep your part of our pact?" he demanded.

Continuing to ignore him, Lara got up and started for the door.

Jake rose and grabbed her arm, spinning her around. "Hold on. I have something to say. And you're going to listen."

Noticing others watching, Lara hesitated. "Say it, then."

Also aware that others were watching, Jake lowered his voice. "Everyone on this planet is pulling together to survive—everyone but you. So far you've done *nothing* to help. Some people think you don't deserve to be here."

"Is that a threat?"

"Call it what you will. I don't care what happens to you. That wasn't part of our agreement. But the child was."

Pulling free of Jake's grasp, Lara again turned to go.

"Jesus, how can you be so selfish?" Jake demanded. "Even for a cyborg, you're—"

"Cyborg?" sputtered a burly, red-faced man sitting nearby. "So it's true!"

"This is between her and me, pal," Jake warned. "Stay out of it."

The man stood, levering his rawboned frame from the bench. "I reckon if she's a cyborg, it concerns *everybody*."

"See? I told you," another man chimed in. "She's the one they were looking for, the one that escaped from the pleasure house."

The red-faced man moved to block Lara's way, his eyes narrowing as he peered at her face.

"Stay out of this," Jake repeated, stepping between the man and Lara.

The man poked a thick finger into Jake's chest. "It's her, all right. And you're the one who brought her, ain't you?" he added, grabbing a handful of Jake's shirt.

Twisting the larger man's wrist, Jake forced him to his knees. The other colonist who had spoken rushed in from behind, circling Jake's neck with his forearm. Snapping forward at the waist, Jake sent the second man tumbling over his back, dumping him onto his red-faced friend and sending both men crashing to the floor.

With a snarl, the red-faced man came up swinging, plowing into Jake. The other man scrambled to his feet and circled left, once more trying to get behind. Jake retreated and threw a jab. The first man ducked and kept coming, walking into a punishing right that again sent him to the floor. He lay groaning, blood spurting from his nose. Seeing his friend down once again, the second man backed away. As quickly as it had begun, the fight was over.

Caught off guard by the sudden violence, Lara glanced around the room, noticing that many hard eyes were now upon her. Realizing she had once more drawn attention to herself, she headed for the door, determined to minimize the damage.

"Grab the cyborg!" someone hollered.

"Do, and you'll regret it," Jake warned.

Silence.

"Ah, let her go," the red-faced man muttered, rising to his feet. He wiped his bloodied nose with the back of his hand. "We'll decide what to do with her when everyone's present," he added, glowering at Jake. "Till then, where's she gonna go?"

Outside, Lara pulled her coat around her as she struck off into the darkness. Passing through the settlement's outer perimeter, she lowered her head against the wind and trudged across the frozen snowfield. For over an hour she walked steadily, working her way ever higher into the surrounding mountains. At last she stopped to rest on a granite outcrop overlooking the valley. Far below she could see the lights of the settlement. Above, a thousand stars glittered in the night sky.

Sitting in the lee of the rock, Lara drew her legs tightly to her chest. By then the temperature had fallen below zero, and her body was shivering uncontrollably. Ignoring her trembling, she tried to think.

Why hasn't Command sent help?

She had already been among the humans far longer than expected. And the longer she stayed, the more trouble they became. She could eliminate them, but could the shell in which she had cloaked herself survive without them? And if her present form were to perish and her true essence be exposed—even for the instant it took to enter a new host—she risked revealing herself to the Dark Ones.

What now?

Coming up with no answers, Lara finally decided to return to the colony and deal with the humans as the need arose. Shaking worse than ever from the cold, she began descending the rocky slope. Before she had gone a dozen steps, she slipped on a patch of ice. Her feet flew out from under her. Arms flailing, she slid several meters on her back. Then suddenly she was falling! Accelerating through the darkness, she dropped, faster, faster . . .

Seconds later she crashed to the rocks below. She heard a sickening thud and felt a white-hot stab of agony. Then, nothing.

She tried to move. She couldn't. Nor could she see. Blind to the world around her, Lara lay trapped in her body. Is it dead? she wondered. No, that couldn't be it. She was still cloaked, still encased within it.

What, then?

Sending her senses inward, Lara examined her injuries. The damage to her body was extensive: bleeding into the abdomen, broken ribs, a shattered leg. Worse, blood was pooling in her cranial cavity, exerting pressure on the neural tissue contained within, and the photonic circuits there as well. All these injuries she could repair, save one. Without help, she couldn't reposition the jagged portions of bone that were protruding through her thigh. And even if she could, she would still be unable to walk.

Lara lay encased in the cyborg's twisted flesh, wondering how long it would survive. With a plunge of despair, she realized her new body wouldn't last the night.

Nor would she.

*   *   *

Hours passed. Stars wheeled in the sky above as Lara made what repairs she could. Although she soon stopped her body's bleeding, she had barely returned the cyborg to consciousness when she sensed the presence of another human.

She reached out with her mind. It was Jake. Then he was beside her, his hands tending to her injured thigh. "What are you doing?" she asked, able at last to open her eyes.

"Splinting your leg," Jake answered curtly.

"How did you find me?"

"I followed your tracks in the snow. Why are you out here?"

"I needed to think."

"Well, you picked one hell of a place to do it," Jake observed quietly.

Using his belt and several lengths of plastic from his backpack, Jake stabilized the bones of Lara's leg. That done, he lifted her and started down the slope. They made good time for the first few minutes. Once they had cleared the protection of the granite face, however, the full force of the wind hit them, and as Jake fought through the drifts, Lara suddenly realized the risk the human called Jake had taken to save her. Puzzled, she asked, "Why did you come for me?"

Jake remained silent for a long moment. Finally he answered. "Let's just say it's something you wouldn't understand," he replied, refusing to say more.

Just before dawn Jake staggered into the settlement, Lara in his arms. Exhausted, he carried her to the infirmary, finding it deserted. Baffled by the absence of medical staff, he placed Lara on a gurney and went in search of assistance. Eventually he spotted Dr. Madison, one of the colony's younger physicians, exiting the quarantine dome. The medic's eyes were bleary, his face drawn. Evidently noting something urgent in Jake's manner, Dr. Madison straightened. "What now?" he sighed when Jake arrived.

"There's been an accident. My . . . wife is hurt," Jake answered. "She needs help."

Reluctantly, Dr. Madison followed Jack back to the infirmary. Upon arrival, the physician withdrew a penlight and shined it into each of Lara's eyes. Then, as Jake watched, he checked the injuries to Lara's chest and leg, started an IV, covered her with a blanket, and wheeled over a portable N-scope. He fell silent as he examined her internal organs, seeming to become progressively mystified as he worked. Finally he flipped off the machine.

"I don't understand," he said, eyeing Lara curiously. "Except for the broken leg, all her injuries seem to have been healing for at least a week. Was there an earlier injury?"

When neither Lara nor Jake responded, Dr. Madison continued. "I also found a power pack where her spleen is supposed to be, and photonic circuitry grafted in her cranium." He turned to Jake. "This creature is a cyborg, but for the life of me I don't understand how she's functioning without a control collar. And I know it's impossible, but she's four months pregnant. What's going on?"

Lara threw off her blanket and sat up. "My injuries were the result of a fall. None of the rest concerns you. Reposition the bones of my leg. I will do the rest." Glancing at Jake, she added, "Please."

Dr. Madison stared. "You'll do the rest?"

"That is correct."

When Lara didn't explain further, the doctor shrugged. "Fine," he grumbled. "I'll set your leg. As it is, that's all I *can* do right now. I have to get back to the quarantine dome."

"Are there any new developments with the fever cases?" asked Jake, welcoming a change of subject.

"You don't know?" replied the physician. "I thought everyone had heard. Where were you last night?"

"I was busy," Jake answered. "Tell me."

The physician looked away. "Three patients died just after midnight. We've lost four additional colonists since then."

"And?" Jake prodded, sensing there was more.

"This morning, twenty new fever cases turned up."

By the end of the week the number of sick had swelled to over a hundred, with more streaming in daily. Eight days later the casualties reached sixty.

During her recuperation from her fall, Lara thought long and hard about the crisis threatening the settlement. Deciding that her survival was linked, at least for the moment, with that of the humans, she came to a decision. When she could walk, she sought out Dr. Moses, the colony's medical director. At that point, to accommodate the growing patient load and isolate the sick from other colonists, all fever victims were being quarantined in one of the largest domes. Lara found Dr. Moses in a cubicle near the entrance, working in a small space that had been set up as a lab. He was hunched over a workbench, methodically examining a tray of microscopic slides.

Dr. Moses looked up as Lara entered. The medical director appeared haggard, as did the rest of the staff. Round-the-clock work had taken its toll. Worse, despite every precaution, nearly a third of the medical team had also contracted the fever. "What do you want?" the doctor asked brusquely.

"I want to help," said Lara.

"You're the cyborg Dr. Madison treated, aren't you?"

Lara nodded.

Dr. Moses eyed her castless leg. "I thought you had a broken femur."

"The bone is healed."

"I can see that." Baffled, the physician stared at Lara. Then, shaking his head, "I suppose it doesn't matter now. You want to help? Fine. Most people won't come near the isolation dome, and we need all the nursing help we can get. But cyborg or not, you realize that if you go in there, you could become infected, too."

"I could become infected anyway. Is that not correct?"

Dr. Moses nodded glumly. "I suppose so. When can you start?"

"Now. But I can do more than nurse the sick. I know what's causing the disease."

Dr. Moses regarded Lara doubtfully. "Is that right?"

"The pathogen is a rod-shaped particle that's transmitted within another single-celled organism, one that you consider harmless."

"How do you know this?"

"I can see it."

"You can *see* it?"

"Yes. Once inside a host, the particle binds with critical proteins and disrupts their function. Search for the pathogen within the mitochondria of infected cells."

Although skeptical, Dr. Moses was also at his wits' end. Deciding that grasping at straws was better than doing nothing at all, he directed his lab team to investigate Lara's assertion. To his amazement she proved correct, and within twenty-four hours they had isolated the offending organism. Racing against time, they began working on a treatment.

The epidemic lasted seven weeks. A vaccine was eventually developed, but not until the disease had nearly run its course. At winter's end, of the four hundred and ninety-one colonists who had landed on Regula, only seventy-six remained.

*   *   *

The survivors elected to burn their dead.

Lara stood in the darkness, apart from the humans. Across the frozen snowfield she could see Jake and Megan and the others gathered around a funeral pyre they had built. Constructed of wood cut from the surrounding forest, it had taken three days to assemble. Giant logs had been set as corner posts, with interlocking timber placed in between. Measuring seven meters square and eighteen meters high, it stood nearly as tall as the main dome of the colony. Steps of horizontal logs created internal platforms throughout the structure. It was upon these platforms that the colonists laid their dead.

In its latter stages the fever had invariably grown incapacitating, with patients requiring constant attention, and during the epidemic's final weeks Lara had spent countless hours on the ward. Originally her concern had been for her own safety, realizing that she needed the other colonists to survive herself. But as she watched the humans die, something had changed. Although she hadn't understood it, she had felt it more strongly every day. She wanted them to live.

She had been there the day they'd brought in Cameron, and the following day when Megan had carried in their son as well. Later, standing beside Cameron's bed, she had heard him speaking to Jake in a rare moment of consciousness. He asked for Jake's promise to watch over Megan and Adam after he was gone.

"You're not going anywhere," Jake had told him fiercely. "You're going to be fine."

"Jake . . ."

"Cam, stop talking like this. You're gonna be fine."

"Please, Jake. Promise."

And at last Jake placed his hand on Cameron's arm and agreed.

Then Cameron had tried to sit, almost knocking over an IV stand beside his bed. "Is Megan here?" he'd asked.

"She's with Adam," Lara had answered, moving closer. "Shall I get her?"

Cameron nodded weakly, then sank back down.

Lara had found Megan on the far side of the ward, in an area reserved for children. She was kneeling beside a cot, holding the hand of her feverish son. "Cameron is conscious," Lara told her. "Go be with him. I'll stay with Adam."

Megan hesitated, then gave Adam's hand a squeeze and hurried off. Once she had left, Lara gazed down at the child on the cot. He was sleeping fitfully, his clothes soaked with sweat. Placing her hand on his burning forehead, she brushed aside his matted hair. Then, on impulse, she slipped into the child's mind, wanting to comfort him, to soothe his fear.

He was beyond reach. She found only pain and confusion. Suddenly a series of convulsions wracked his body, each more violent than the last. Lara tried to maintain her link with him, but could not. Helplessly, she watched as he arched and shuddered and finally lay still.

Now he rested beside his father in the pyre. Cameron, and Adam, and hundreds more like them.

Lara remained in the darkness as the fire was set. She watched as flames licked up the mountain of timber, illuminating the faces of the encircling humans. They stood together holding hands, somber and dry-eyed, slowly drawing back as the flames raged higher. How fragile these beings are, she thought once again. But as she regarded them in the flickering light, she also realized that there was more to them than she had first suspected.

Slowly, she walked forward and joined the circle. Taking Jake's hand, she stood with the humans, watching as the fire blazed into the night. And deep within her, she felt the precious spark of life she had started begin to move.

Spring came at last. The snows slowly withdrew up the mountain slopes, and the valley bloomed with life. Under a crystalline blue sky, Jake and Lara sat on the granite crag where Lara had nearly lost her life the previous winter. Together they gazed out over the land. The valley below was now thick with waist-high grasses that rolled and swept in the wind, moving like an ocean of green in the morning sun. Flowers dotted the hillsides to the south; to the east a river shimmered through a wall of trees guarding its flanks.

Fed by rushing cascades, the river had swollen during spring thaw, flooding the lowlands near the colony before finally receding. From their rocky perch, Lara and Jake watched it flow, tracing the course of the valley as it collected in lazy pools here and there, rushing in the narrows and fanning out in wider sections on its meander to the sea. On its western bank several fields were now under cultivation, and young animals—pigs, sheep, cows, and horses from the colony's library of frozen livestock embryos—frisked in bordering grasslands and pens.

Most of the other colonists were absent, having departed to begin a ground survey of the planet. Mechanized farming required the efforts of only a few, and Jake and Lara and a handful of others had elected to stay. Turning from the view below, Lara glanced at the human beside her. Resisting a desire to touch him, she placed a hand on her swollen abdomen, thinking back to the night after the funeral. Not wanting to be alone, she had followed Jake back to his quarters. He'd seemed uneasy, and she had asked if he objected to her presence.

"I'm not sure how I feel right now," he'd responded. "We haven't been alone together since . . ."

"Since back on Earth? Since the night I took this body?"

Jake nodded.

"I regret what happened then. I mistakenly thought you were attacking me. Later I realized you were simply indulging in the mating process. Speaking of which, there is something about that I still don't understand. When I first took this body, it had been altered and was incapable of reproduction. The data in my memory banks explained what you were doing, but not *why*."

"Reproduction isn't the only purpose of the mating process, as you put it."

"Oh? What else is there?"

"Well, for one thing, sex can be used to show love and affection."

"Why would you want to show love and affection for someone you've never met, especially a cyborg? And why was the transfer of money necessary?"

"Let's just say it seemed like a good idea at the time."

"Please, Jake. I'm trying to understand."

"Okay," Jake sighed. He thought a moment. "Remember eating breakfast this morning?"

"Mmmm, yes. Scrambled protein, rehydrated potatoes, pancakes, and coffee. It was delicious."

"Right. Your body needs food, so it's happy when it gets fed. Sex is similar. You can be hungry for that, too. If you reexamine your memory, you'll find that sex doesn't necessarily have to be unpleasant."

"It can be pleasurable, too? Like food?" Curious, Lara referred to the cyborg's basic operating program. To her amazement, she discovered there *was* something she had overlooked.

"Jake, will you do something for me?" she asked.

"What?"

"May we try it one more time? Please?"

Hours later Lara stretched lazily, rolling away from Jake's comforting warmth. Sitting up in bed, she watched him as he slept, then shook him gently. "Jake?"

"Huh?"

"Are you conscious?"

"I am now."

"Good. I'm hungry. May we eat?"

"I think I can handle that," Jake had answered with a grin.

"And Jake? Afterward . . . let's do it again."

Now, as Jake and Lara sat on the outcrop above the settlement, white puffs of clouds began forming over the land, casting a moving patchwork of light and shadow across the hills below. Warmed by the sun, Lara gazed over the valley, noticing a foxlike animal moving stealthily through the fields. She studied it for several minutes, then nudged Jake. "There's something down there," she said, pointing.

Jake squinted, catching a glimpse of the predator slipping through the grass. "I've seen a couple of those around lately," he said. "They look like a cross between a fox and a cat."

Moments later the creature disappeared, showing itself again briefly as it crossed a clearing.

"What's it doing?"

"Hunting, probably," Jake answered with a shrug. Then, dismissing the animal, "It's beautiful here, isn't it?"

"Yes, it is," Lara answered, surprised to find that she truly meant it.

"What's it like where you come from?"

Lara considered carefully. "It's hard to explain in terms you could comprehend."

"Try."

"Well, it's beautiful there, too," she said, again catching sight of the fox. "There's life, so much life. Not like here, but . . . it's beautiful there, too."

Jake and Lara fell silent once more, continuing to track the fox as it crept through the fields. As it neared the base of the mountain, a bird appeared, hovering in the currents above the valley floor. It hung in an updraft a moment, then abruptly folded its wings and dived at the fox, pulling up at the last second. Seeming injured, it fluttered to the ground thirty meters from the predator.

The fox changed direction. Before it reached its prey, the downed bird rose again, only to fall once more near a stand of trees bordering the field. "Is it hurt?" Lara asked as the bird barely escaped a second time.

"I don't think so," Jake answered. "It looks as though it's trying to draw the fox away. Probably has a nest in that field somewhere."

"But it's risking its own life."

"Animals often do that to protect their young." Jake placed a hand on Lara's abdomen. "Speaking of which, how's it doing?"

"He," Lara said. "The child is male."

"How do you—" Jake shook his head. "Never mind. I should know better by now. How soon will he come?"

"Soon," Lara answered. "I've accelerated his growth and made other changes as well. He'll be a very special human. At present he is fully formed and eager to see his new world. He says he is eager to meet you, too."

"You *talk* with him?"

"Of course. I want him to remember me after I'm gone."

Jake regarded her carefully. "Gone? What do you mean?"

"You know that my people are looking for me. When they arrive, I must depart."

"But . . . do you really have to leave? Can't you—"

"No," Lara interrupted, taking Jake's hand. "I'm a soldier, bound by duty to return."

"But . . ."

"I'm sorry, Jake. It's out of my control."

Jake nodded. "I guess I knew you would have to leave sometime. I just . . ." His voice trailed off.

"I will miss you," said Lara, surprised by the depth of her feeling.

"I'll miss you, too."

"No matter what happens, I won't leave until the child is born," Lara promised, a sudden emptiness welling within.

Again Jake nodded, not trusting himself to speak.

"Another transport vessel will arrive and you can leave with your son, if that is your wish," Lara continued. "You and your child can return to Earth. You don't have to be alone."

"I'm not going anywhere." Jake entwined his fingers in Lara's, then forced a smile. "There's nothing for me on Earth anymore. I belong here. Besides, the next transport won't even be sent until the *Patriot* confirms the placement of our colony. Assuming they dispatch another vessel immediately, it will be years before it arrives."

"Years? But the trip only took twenty-two days."

"Twenty-two days—*ship's time.* While we were in transit, over eighteen years passed on Earth. You know the relativistic effect that warp travel has on time."

"No," Lara replied, shaken by Jake's words. "I didn't."

Later that night, Lara lay awake long after Jake had fallen asleep. She could hear him breathing softly beside her. Outside the wind had picked up, and the sound of it rushing through the trees reached her before she felt it buffet their dome. Repeatedly, her thoughts returned to Jake's revelation on the hillside. Including the time they had spent in transit, over eighteen years had passed since she entered this continuum. True, the arrow of time moved more swiftly here than on her home plane, but *eighteen years*? Why hadn't she been contacted? And where was the enemy? Had her failure to complete her mission resulted in some disastrous outcome for her race?

She could wait no longer. Regardless of the risk, she had to know.

Tentatively, she opened her mind and examined the swirl of stars that surrounded her, instantaneously traversing the boundaries of space and time. She found nothing.

Could the Dark Ones have abandoned their search?

Hoping against hope, she next turned her attention to a neighboring galaxy known to the humans as Andromeda. She recoiled from what she discovered. Inexplicably, hundreds of stars had been reduced to glowing shells of incandescent gas. Only shattered remnants marked their previous existence. One by one, she visited other galaxies in the local cluster. Some were as yet untouched, but many had suffered the same catastrophic fate as Andromeda. As she watched, a sun in a nearby elliptical galaxy blossomed, incinerating its attendant planets in a cataclysmic explosion of light.

At last Lara understood. Appalled, she pulled in the tendrils of her mind. She had counted over three hundred supernovae in Andromeda alone, and many more in other galaxies. Normally, stellar explosions occurred only rarely, coming at the end of a star's life. These explosions hadn't happened naturally. With a feeling of profound horror and regret and shame, she realized they were because of her.

Despite her fear of being discovered, Lara again opened her mind and called for help.

Minutes later she shook Jake. "Wake up!"

"What's the matter?" Jake mumbled groggily. Then, suddenly alert, "The baby? Is it time?"

"That's not it. Look at me. There's something I must show you."

Puzzled, Jake peered into the widening pools of Lara's eyes. As before, he saw into her mind, this time gazing upon the unthinkable destruction that had taken place in galaxies millions of light years distant. "All those stars exploding . . . What's going on?" he asked shakily.

"I told you the Dark Ones were hunting me," Lara answered. "Each of the shattered suns you see once supported a planetary system that was home to intelligent life. Instead of searching among those life forms for me, they simply exploded the primary star, incinerating everything in the system."

"But why?"

"To winnow me out. Upon destroying all organic life near the star, I would be the only one left."

"But causing a star to explode. How is that possible?"

Lara shrugged. "It's a simple matter to enter a sun and disrupt the delicate balance between its gravitational contraction and the radiation pressure from its core."

"Enter a star? You can do that?"

"Not while confined to this body. But yes, I can do that. As can they."

Jake passed his hand over his face, stunned by Lara's words. Entire races annihilated, solar systems destroyed . . . because of her.

"There's more," Lara continued somberly. "I just contacted my headquarters. They're not coming for me. It seems the information I'm carrying is false. From the very first, I was intended to fall into enemy hands. I was meant to be a sacrifice."

"You're not going through with it, are you?" Jake demanded angrily.

Lara glanced away. "No. I won't give my life, not for them. But now that I've revealed myself, the Dark Ones will soon arrive. I can escape, but I must leave immediately."

"Lara—"

"There is no time for discussion," Lara interrupted. "I need your help. When I vacate this body, it will cease to function. You must take the child now." She walked to their dome's medical cabinet, searched through the first-aid canister, and returned with a scalpel. "Cut him out," she said, extending the knife to Jake.

Realizing what she was asking, Jake shook his head. "Lara, I can't—"

"You have to. I know what to do. I need your hands to do it."

Jake backed away. "I'll . . . I'll get the doctor," he stammered.

"There is no time. My enemies will be here in minutes. It must be done now."

Once more Jake looked into Lara's eyes and knew, beyond a doubt, that she was telling the truth. He tried to find another way, but couldn't. As if in a dream, he watched as she lay on the bed. Then the knife was in his hand and Lara was in his mind, and he knew what he had to do.

Fighting to control his trembling, Jake opened Lara's bedclothes and made the first incision, drawing the scalpel down the midline of her abdomen. Like paint from a brush, a bright trail of red welled up behind the blade. Again he cut, and again, dissecting through layers of skin and muscle and fascia. Through

Lara's mindlink he could feel a shadow of the pain she was enduring. Afraid to look at her face, he focused his attention on the task before him.

Sweat beading his brow, Jake made a final incision through the tough muscular wall of the uterus, cutting where Lara instructed. Clear fluid suddenly washed the wound. He could see the infant, tangled in the umbilical cord. With shaking hands, he reached into the glistening membranes. Carefully, he withdrew the child and brought it into the world.

A perfect baby! A boy!

Seconds later the stillness was broken by the sound of the infant's cry.

After tying and cutting the cord, Jake knelt beside the bed. By then the child had stopped crying, and his pale blue eyes were open and alert. "May I hold him?" Lara whispered.

Overcome with emotion, Jake placed the baby in Lara's arms. "What do you want to call him?" he asked softly.

Lara looked up. "If you agree," she answered, "I would like to name him Adam."

Jake nodded, his vision blurring. "Cameron would have liked that. I think Megan will approve, too." Then, taking Lara's hand, "Tell me something, Lara. Please. I have to know."

"What?"

Jake swallowed, trying to find words to voice a question that had plagued him from the very beginning. "I know that creating our child was a means for you to escape, at least at first," he said. "Once we left Earth, you could have stopped the child whenever you wanted. Why didn't you?"

Lara thought back to the first moment she had first gazed upon this universe. Then, life had meant nothing more to her than a clever arrangement of molecules and atoms. Now, holding the tiny being she had created, she knew that to express her feelings would require far longer than the few seconds she had left. "I don't know," she said, her eyes shining, a smile playing across her lips. "To quote a very special human, let's just say that it seemed like a good idea at the time. And it was."

Lara squeezed Jake's hand. Then her fingers opened . . . and she was gone.

She waited for them among the stars, fighting the compulsion to flee. Although she could not yet see the enemy, she felt them approaching. She could also feel their hate, and she was afraid.

On the edge of the galaxy's nearest arm, she could make out a tiny point of light called Regula. She regarded it one last time, and the planet circling fourth from the center. Her thoughts returned briefly to a bird she had once watched there, moving through a grassy field. Then she resumed her vigil.

There! She could see the Dark Ones now. As expected, they were arrowing directly for the Regula system and the star at its center, intent on their strategy of incineration.

As death hurtled closer, she unfolded her fields, and the interstellar vastness pulsed and coursed and shimmered with the energy of her essence. Still, they did not see her. Fighting her terror, she forced herself to move closer. Suddenly the Dark Ones hesitated. Faltering as if in distress, she turned to flee. Looking back, she saw them veer from Regula, now coming straight for her.

She had no illusions concerning her chance of escape. The time for that had long since passed. Capture was inevitable. Capture, and death. Yet still she fled—drawing away the enemy from Regula—hoping the end would be easy, knowing it would not.

Her final thoughts were of Adam.

Jake stood beside the still form on the bed. Lara appeared peaceful now, at rest. Reaching down, he brushed back a lock of hair from her forehead, then gently closed her eyes and lifted the child from her lifeless embrace. Adam was sleeping, his breath coming easily.

What am I to do with him? Jake wondered numbly. Thinking of Megan, he bundled the infant in a blanket and moved to the door. It was still dark outside, but a faint glow on the horizon heralded the coming dawn. Noticing something odd in the sky, Jake paused in the doorway.

Shining like a beacon, a strange star traveled the constellations, burning more brightly than any around it. All at once it swelled, grew dazzlingly brilliant, and died to an ember. As it grew dim Jake looked down, noticing that Adam had awakened and was watching, too. The child stared into the heavens until the errant star had disappeared. Then he turned his eyes to Jake. Solemnly, he raised a tiny hand to touch his father's cheek. And with a flood of comprehension, Jake understood what had happened. He knew what Lara had done, and why, and what it had cost her.

A breeze moved up the valley, carrying with it the smells of the fields and the scent of pine and the sounds of the colony's livestock waking in their pens. For a long moment Jake stood in the doorway, his mind filled with thoughts of Lara, a stranger from another universe who had given him a child, and a beautiful new world, and in the end, her life.

As light broke over the settlement, Jake turned and gazed one last time at the still form on the bed. Then, holding his son safe in his arms, filled with a sense of sadness and wonder and a deep, abiding gratitude for the mystery of life, he stepped out to face the dawn.

There's Always a Catch

Dr. Isaac Greenbaum paced the cramped confines of the television-studio waiting room. Struggling to ignore a premonition of disaster that had settled like a stone in the pit of his stomach, he contemplated the probable consequences of his upcoming news announcement. People being what they were, he suspected that he would undoubtedly tumble from his position as the most honored scientist on Earth, instead becoming one of the most reviled.

How did things go so wrong? he wondered miserably. Only days before he had been preparing his research for publication. Then, against his will, he'd become an object of adulation, a situation for which, however flattering, he had been totally unprepared.

Then his real problems began.

Glancing around the claustrophobic cubicle in which they had deposited him to await the broadcast, he spotted yesterday's newspaper on the coffee table. In bold banner letters, a single word blazed across the top of page one: IMMORTALITY!

Damn TriBionics, he thought angrily. And damn the media for spreading their premature announcements to every corner of the world. Of course, TriBionic stock had soared following the press release. Great for shareholders, but *his* would be the name that was remembered when the truth finally came out.

"Dr. Greenbaum?"

Dr. Greenbaum turned, finding himself facing the most dazzlingly beautiful woman he had ever seen. "Uh, yes?"

"I'm Rhonda Davidson," the woman said, extending her hand. "It's an honor to meet you, Doctor."

Her grasp was warm and firm. As he shook her hand, Dr. Greenbaum forced himself to stop gawking. He had seen the newswoman many times on television, but in person she was even more striking than she was on TV—tall, poised, beautiful—and possessing a directness of manner in her on-air interviews that he had always found attractive.

"The network appreciates your granting us this exclusive interview," Ms. Davidson continued, checking her watch. "We still have some time before the broadcast. I thought perhaps we could get to know each other a bit before then. Perhaps talk about the interview." Pulling a packet of index cards from her pocket, she moved to the couch. Patting a cushion, she indicated for him to join her.

Attempting to hide his nervousness, Dr. Greenbaum sat. "Ms. Davidson, I agreed to—"

"Please. Call me Rhonda."

"All right. Rhonda. I agreed to appear on your newscast with the caveat that I be allowed to make a personal statement. You understand this?"

"I understand your request," said Rhonda, glancing at her cards. "Of course, I have to ask what you plan to say. We can't just—"

"No statement, no interview."

Rhonda quickly backtracked. "No, that's all right, Doctor. You . . . you can make your statement. But is there some reason you can't tell me what it involves? It *is* regarding your regeneration therapy, right?"

"Yes."

"Then why—"

Dr. Greenbaum raised his hand. "No offense, but I'm not in a very trusting mood at the moment. Without my permission—without even consulting me, for that matter—you and others in the media have made public the results of my research. Through no fault of mine certain elements were ignored, elements I want understood by everyone equally and at the same time. This will be a worldwide broadcast, correct?"

Rhonda nodded. "We're transmitting live. Practically every man, woman, and child on the planet with access to the internet will be watching."

"Good."

Rhonda regarded Dr. Greenbaum quizzically. Then, realizing he intended to say nothing more on the subject, she pocketed her cards, rose from the couch, and again glanced at her watch. "Air time is in five minutes, Doctor. Shall we?"

". . . extremely fortunate to have with us the researcher who is responsible for the recent breakthrough in regenerative biotechnology, Dr. Isaac Greenbaum. Thank you for joining us today, Doctor. Perhaps you could begin by telling us how you came to unlock the secret of aging?"

Dr. Greenbaum squinted into the studio lights. A battery of cameras stared back, thickets of cables traversing the floor in all directions. Nervously, Dr. Greenbaum returned his gaze to Rhonda, who was seated across from him at a low table. "Of course," he said, deciding to put off his announcement for the moment.

"You began in cancer research?"

"That's right. In many ways, my regeneration discoveries were serendipitous."

"They were accidental? How so?"

"Well, curiously enough, the two subjects are closely related," Dr. Greenbaum explained, feeling his nervousness beginning to dissipate as he moved into familiar territory. "First let me give you a little background. Many primitive cells possess the ability to replicate indefinitely and are, in a sense, immortal. In more complex organisms like man, cells specialize to perform specific functions for the benefit of the whole. Unfortunately, the more specialized a cell is, the less readily it is able to reproduce. A human neuron, for instance, almost completely lacks that ability."

"And being able to replicate indefinitely means immortality?"

"Yes, if you're referring to a single-celled organism. In a multicellular animal like man, it's not that simple. Some tissues in our bodies already replace themselves constantly—skin cells, for example—yet still they age in time.

"And how does your cancer research bear on this?"

"A cancer, or neoplastic growth, starts from a single cell in which the molecular machinery governing replication goes awry, permitting it to grow unchecked." Dr. Greenbaum paused, recalling that Rhonda had cautioned him to keep his scientific explanations short. "What caught my attention was that a neoplasm often arises from highly specialized tissues that previously lacked the ability to reproduce," he continued, doing his best to abbreviate his response. "In pursuing this area I discovered the Aging Triad—three separate genes that govern the aging process in every cell of our bodies. From there it was a straightforward matter to develop blocking enzymes that induce regeneration and prevent aging."

Dr. Greenbaum hesitated, sensing that he had lost Rhonda toward the end.

"In other words, you've unlocked the secret of immortality," Rhonda pushed ahead, filling the breach. "You must be extremely proud of your work and the benefit it promises mankind," she added, moving smoothly to her next topic.

Dr. Greenbaum's brow furrowed. "At first, yes. Now I'm not so sure."

"I don't understand. You've given the world the gift of life. From a personal standpoint, let me say that the possibility of never aging, of living forever, has changed the way I look at things. It's as if an invisible weight has been lifted from my shoulders. I can't begin to describe it."

Dr. Greenbaum leaned closer. "Let me ask you something, Rhonda. Do you have children?"

"No."

"Do you plan to?"

Puzzled, Rhonda shrugged. "Someday, maybe. Why?"

"Consider this. What will life on Earth be like a hundred years from now? Two hundred? Three hundred? Will life be worth living when your children, and their children, and their children's children choke the face of our planet—and no one has died to make room?"

Rhonda frowned, sensing the interview veering in a direction she hadn't anticipated. "We'll find a solution," she answered confidently. "Mandatory birth control, perhaps. Space travel to new worlds. Whatever."

"Possibly. But there's a more serious problem. Man's very existence arose from a process of natural selection. Life evolves through random variations, with members of each new generation possibly better suited to a changing environment. I fear that the application of my findings will result in a complete genetic stagnation of our race."

"You can't be suggesting that we ignore your breakthrough," Rhonda objected.

"No. For better or worse, TriBionics will, for a price, make the results of my work available to all mankind."

Rhonda brightened. "That's a relief. Just exactly how—"

"I want to add something here," Dr. Greenbaum interrupted, deciding the time had come for honesty. He took a deep breath and let it out slowly. Turning to speak directly to the camera, he addressed the peoples of the world. "My reason for being here today is to apologize for the premature release of my research," he said. "An important aspect has not yet been made public. It is my duty to do so now."

He hesitated, then forged ahead, speaking slowly and deliberately. "In every mammalian organism studied to date, *including man*, the Aging Triad has proved to be irreversibly activated during early embryonic development."

"What does that mean?" asked Rhonda. "In layman's terms?"

Everyone in the studio waited for Dr. Greenbaum to continue. And with them the world waited as well, hoping against hope. But deep down, everyone already suspected the truth. It was something our race had learned long ago, a truth that time and experience had burned into our collective consciousness: No matter how good something sounds at first . . . there's *always* a catch.

"The immortality treatments must begin in utero, at least seven months prior to birth," said Dr. Greenbaum. "We can offer our future children the gift of immortality. They and those coming after them will have the chance to live forever, God help them. But not us. Not us."

"But . . ."

129

"I'm sorry." Dr. Greenbaum lowered his head. "Our generation—everyone now living and those about to be born—will be the last to grow old," he said softly. "Others may live forever, but we will not. We will be the last to die."

The Crux

I have made some monumental blunders in my life, and it looked like I had just made another. Though I didn't understand why, one thing was quickly becoming clear: I shouldn't have laughed at Bellagorski.

"You think I'm funny, Spencer?" he growled, his eyes glittering with rage.

The sun had just broken over the ridge to the east, draping long, ominous shadows across our campsite. Bellagorski was sitting beside the dying embers in the fire ring. From the look of his bloodshot eyes—not to mention an empty fifth of tequila and a pile of beer cans littering the sand beside his bedroll—he appeared to have been up all night. When I didn't reply, I noticed that his huge, rawboned fists were clenched knuckle-white at his sides. Not for the first time that morning, the realization struck me that Bellagorski looked exactly like what he was—a mean, dangerous, egocentric son of a bitch.

Jack Wolfe, my climbing partner, and I had met Bellagorski in Yosemite three months back. He'd been climbing solo . . . unroped. I hadn't liked him right from the start, but for some reason Jack had let him tie with us over the next couple of days. As I got to know Bellagorski better, I liked him even less, but one thing I won't deny. He could climb.

Jack and I had a week's trip to Joshua Tree National Monument planned for later that fall. To my irritation, Jack had invited Bellagorski to join us; then at the last minute Jack canceled. I decided to go anyway, figuring *some* climbing was better than none, even if it was with a jerk like Bellagorski.

I couldn't have been more wrong.

I had left work early the day before, making good time on the drive out from L.A. I passed the Palm Springs turnoff in just under two hours, then headed east on Route 62 and climbed into the high desert of Morongo Valley toward Joshua Tree. My dog, J.R., was sitting shotgun, as usual. When Susan (my wife of five years) and I had separated last January, we had each taken what we loved. She'd grabbed the condo. I had taken J.R.

Late that afternoon I pulled into the Hidden Valley Campground. By then the sun had begun its descent, but the desert was still plenty hot, and J.R. had been hanging her head out the window for the past few hours trying to cool down. Glad to stretch my legs, I cut the engine, stepped to the back of my Jeep, and opened the hatch to give her some water. As I filled her bowl from a five-gallon army-surplus can, I spotted Bellagorski's beat-up van parked beside the camp bulletin board. I glanced around. Most of the campsites were deserted. Bellagorski was nowhere in sight.

Curious, I checked across the road, noting a small group of people clustered around the base of Intersection Rock. They were watching a lone figure about 150 feet up, climbing unroped.

Bellagorski.

I walked over, never taking my eyes from the rock face. Bellagorski was nearing the top, having nearly completed a difficult route called North Overhang. As he progressed, his body flowed effortlessly from hold to hold, each of his moves deliberate, fluid, controlled. I craned my neck with the others, squinting into the sun. Everyone there stared spellbound as Bellagorski approached the crux, the most difficult part of the climb. I had done the route several times, and I knew the crux involved a demanding series of moves to surmount a large overhang. Unroped, one tiny slip meant death.

Bellagorski hesitated, then started up again. He hung briefly by one hand, then pushed off the face and swung out over the drop, making a dynamic slap for the last critical hold. An instant later he had his feet back on the rock . . . and he scrambled to top.

He made it look easy.

That night Bellagorski and I camped at the foot of a huge unnamed wall that Jack and I had discovered the previous spring. I had suggested to Bellagorski that we give it a try the following morning, and he'd agreed. We were in a closed area about fifteen miles down an abandoned mining road, far from the park campgrounds. We weren't supposed to be there, but the rangers rarely traveled that far out without a reason. For the most part, nobody else did, either.

We ate in silence. Afterward we sat around the fire watching the stars come out. Despite the poor company, it felt good being away from the city. Before long Bellagorski started drinking. I wouldn't say alcohol exactly loosened him up, but at least it got him talking. "Why'd you pull that stunt this afternoon?" I asked when the conversation turned to climbing.

"Why do you think?" he replied, giving the coals a kick that sent a shower of sparks spinning into the night.

"I don't know," I answered. And I didn't. Over the years, most of the guys I had roped up with considered me a pretty fair climber. Jack and I have put up several new routes in Joshua Tree and Idyllwild, even one in Yosemite. Nonetheless, I considered the unroped ascent of a difficult technical climb just plain showboating, pure and simple. "Maybe you have a death wish," I ventured.

"Shows what you know. Lemme ask you something, hotshot. Why do *you* climb?"

I shrugged. "All the obvious reasons."

"Like?"

"Like the challenge, solving technical problems, the feeling I get at the top."

"Bull. That's not why you climb. That's just the window dressing."

"Okay, you tell me. Why do I climb?"

"Simple. It's the thrill. You climb for the same reason that even some schmuck businessman can't resist edging up to the window on the sixty-seventh floor of his office building and looking down, even though he's crappin' his pants the whole time. It's the thrill that's got you hooked, Spencer. It's the adrenaline rush of death staring you in the face. *That's* why you climb."

"Maybe that's true, at least in part," I reluctantly agreed. "But using a rope minimizes the chances of actually *dying*. You're insane to climb without one."

Bellagorski's face darkened. "You gutless puke, don't *ever* call me that. You're like some old lady who's afraid to hang her ass on the line. Guys like you make me sick."

We talked on into the night. Argued, mostly. Bellagorski snorted some coke and kept on drinking. And the more he drank, the more our conversation degenerated. Eventually I decided to turn in, resolving to return to the park in the morning—figuring I could still do a little bouldering, possibly even find another climbing partner. Anyone but Bellagorski.

When I awoke, Bellagorski picked up where we had left off the night before, seeming determined to escalate our disagreement to a whole new level. He was drunk, and I didn't take him seriously. I even made the mistake of laughing at him. But when I noticed the expression on his face and the manic glint in his eyes, I decided it was time to get the hell out.

"You think I'm funny?" he demanded again.

"There's absolutely nothing funny about you, asshole," I said. "C'mon, J.R. Let's go." As J.R. trotted over, I tossed the dregs of my coffee into the fire and turned my back. It was my second mistake of the morning.

J.R. probably saved my life. I heard a low rumbling deep in her throat. I glanced back and saw Bellagorski rushing me from behind. I threw up an arm without thinking, taking most of the blow on my forearm. Numbing pain shot up to my shoulder.

I backed away, warily watching Bellagorski. He had my short-handled latrine shovel gripped in both hands. Wielding it like an ax, he swung again. I stumbled, narrowly evading the blade as it flashed past my face. Continuing my retreat, I peered around the campsite, searching for a weapon. There was nothing.

Still growling, J.R. circled to the left. Bellagorski's eyes were riveted on me, but I could tell part of his attention was on her, too. J.R. is a big dog—malamute and shepherd mix. She's also harmless, but Bellagorski didn't know that.

"J.R., get him!" I yelled.

Bellagorski took his eyes off me for an instant. That's all it took. I moved in. He swung, but by then I had slipped inside the arc of his shovel. The handle glanced off my shoulder. I grabbed a fistful of shirt. Before he could swing the shovel again, I threw my left.

I connected. Something in Bellagorski's face crunched under my knuckles. With a mingling of rage and fear, I hit him again. His legs buckled. The shovel dropped from his hands. Blood streamed from his nose, but he wouldn't go down. Bellowing in anger, he ripped free of my grasp and wiped his hand across his mouth, gaping in disbelief at his bloody palm. Then his eyes narrowed. He spat on the ground and charged, attempting to encircle me with his arms.

I retreated, staying just out of range. I couldn't let him take the fight to the ground, where his size and weight would quickly end it. He was drunk, but still a lot stronger than I was.

The shovel forgotten, he continued to stalk me, a mist of blood spraying from his mouth with each breath. The next time he rushed me I jabbed once, stepped to the right, and dropped. With a hooking motion of my right foot, I swept his legs out from under him.

He went down. Hard.

Normally I wouldn't hit a guy when he's flat on his back. I made an exception for Bellagorski. As he lay gasping for breath, I put my knee on his chest and slammed my fist into his face till he stopped moving.

Leaving him bleeding, I gathered my things as quickly as I could. I had just finished stowing my sleeping bag and cook kit in the back of my Jeep when he rose and stumbled to his van. I grabbed my rope, slings, and equipment rack, then made one last check of the camp. I didn't plan on coming back.

As I was loading the last of my climbing gear, Bellagorski reemerged from his van. He started toward me. He had a gun.

With a flick of his wrist, he motioned me away from the Jeep.

I didn't move. "What do you think you're doing?"

"Shut up." Once more he motioned with the pistol, then pointed it at me. I moved.

"Put on your climbing shoes," he ordered.

"Why?"

"Get 'em on," he hissed, speaking with difficulty. His mouth was a mess. I had broken some teeth.

I sat in the dirt, removed my boots, and pulled on my climbing shoes. As I began lacing them, J.R. lay beside me, acting confused. "It's okay, girl," I said quietly, wishing it were true. She thumped the ground a couple times with her tail.

After I had laced my shoes, I stood and faced Bellagorski. "Now what? You gonna shoot me?"

His tongue flicked across his puffy lips. "Don't think I won't," he warned, his eyes shifting to the towering rock wall behind me. "It wouldn't be the first time."

Seconds ticked by, seeming like hours. I stood, sweat gathering under my arms. I suddenly realized that I knew nothing about Bellagorski—not his first name, or where he lived, or even a phone number. Nothing. And right then, he looked capable of *anything*, even cold-blooded murder.

It wouldn't be the first time, he'd said. I remembered the shovel, wondering whether he would have stopped with the first blow. I held my breath, expecting at any moment to see the gun jump in his hand and feel the stab of a bullet tearing into my chest.

At last he spoke. "I'm gonna give you a chance to learn something about yourself, hotshot," he said coldly, still glancing at the wall. Then he grinned, his eyes as hard as diamonds. "Climb it."

I looked at the rock face. It rose almost vertically from the desert floor for most of its five-hundred-foot ascent. Nothing broke its surface for the first two hundred feet; then a system of cracks led to a slot that continued to just below the summit, ending an overhanging roof. As far as I knew, the wall had never been climbed. Jack and I had made two abortive runs at it earlier that summer, and after those attempts I had begun to suspect that it couldn't be done—at least by us. One thing I did know: To attempt it unroped would be suicide.

I shook my head. "No way."

Bellagorski's grin got even uglier. "Maybe I didn't make myself clear. I'm not asking you. I'm *telling* you."

"Or you'll shoot me."

"You don't think I will?"

I didn't answer. By then sweat had soaked through my shirt. My arm was throbbing from the shovel blow. We stood, our eyes locked. Then Bellagorski lowered his gun and shot J.R.

She squealed once and crumpled to the ground. I knelt beside her, my ears ringing from the blast. He had shot her through the back. Her teeth bared in pain, she began to convulse, whimpering pitifully as her life spilled out onto the sand. "No, no, no," I whispered, my vision blurring. I held her head in my lap, powerless to keep her from slipping away.

The shot echoed across the valley, returning again and again before dying away. I rose, choked with hate for the man before me. Bellagorski laughed, once more leveling the pistol at my chest. At that moment if I'd had Bellagorski's gun, I swear I would have blown him away without thinking. But I didn't have the gun. *He* did. And if I didn't do what he wanted, I knew he would use it on me.

Before an ascent, the minutes spent at the base of a climb are always a nervous time for me. Uncoiling the rope, going through the equipment rack, studying the rock, and referring to the guidebook, if there is one, usually gives me a chance to settle down and get the proper mindset. Because the sum total of my equipment now consisted of climbing shoes and a chalk bag on a sling, I didn't even have that.

"Get moving," Bellagorski snarled.

I looked up. The stone seemed to rise forever. For a sickening instant I had the impression that at any moment it might come crashing down upon me. Briefly I considered trying to run. A field of boulders offered shelter to my left, but to get there I would have to cross seventy-five yards of open desert. I'd never make it. Reluctantly, I placed my hand on the wall.

It felt rough. As were most of the granitic formations in the area, it was composed of quartz monzonite. The large crystals embedded in it were tough on hands and equipment, but ideal for friction climbing.

I started up.

Progressing quickly, I ascended on seemingly impossible flakes and nubbins. Because of the coarse nature of the rock, they were more than adequate . . . at first. About forty feet up I reached the initial bolt Jack and I had placed for protection on our previous attempt. I regarded it longingly, wishing I could clip in. Searching the rock face above, I spotted the second bolt. Higher up was a third, the final one we'd placed. Neither Jack nor I had made it much past that third bolt.

I held no illusions about my ability to complete the climb. Nonetheless, I hoped that if I could progress past the third bolt without falling, I had a chance of reaching the crack system higher up. And from there, the vertical chimney above it. If I made it to the chimney, I planned on wedging myself in and waiting for help to arrive. But first I had to get there.

Above the first bolt, the climbing increased in difficulty. I kept going, but fifteen feet below the second bolt I froze. I couldn't go on. My right leg, which at that point was supporting most of my weight, started trembling.

Relax, I told myself. *If you think this is bad, wait until after the third bolt.*

Thanks for the encouragement. I needed that.

Would you rather go down and face a bullet?

No.

Then climb.

I chalked my hands and climbed—moving carefully, trying not to think about the ever-increasing drop beneath me. I passed the second bolt.

As near as I could judge, I had been on the face about three quarters of an hour when I reached the third bolt. By then our camp lay far below. My red Cherokee, its hatch still open, sat like a toy in the morning sun. I could see Bellagorski lounging in a folding chair by the fire ring, watching me. He still had the gun in his hand. I could hear him laughing.

"You're committed now, hotshot," he hollered up, his voice rising through the clear desert air.

I knew what he meant. I had been trying not to think about it. Face climbing is a delicate, deliberate process of moving a single hand or foot in turn, carefully exchanging handholds for footholds, always moving up. Climbing *down* is generally more difficult. For one thing, you can't always see where you're placing your feet. For another, what works on the way up often fails miserably on the way down. In fact, past a certain technical difficulty it's *impossible* to down-climb a route you've just ascended.

And you're way past that point now, my internal voice reminded me.

I reached the spot where I'd peeled on my attempt with Jack the preceding spring. Far above I could see the crack system leading to the chimney. It took every ounce of will I possessed to venture on. Instead of climbing directly toward the cracks as I had on my earlier attempt, I traversed left across the face before continuing up, trying another approach. It worked. Twenty minutes later, climbing better than I ever had in my life, I reached a tiny ledge just below the first cracks. Pausing to catch my breath, I considered the best way to proceed.

Suddenly the rock wall exploded beside me!

Flying shards of stone stung my face, momentarily blinding me. A split second later I heard the sound of a gunshot thundering up from below.

My concentration broke. I felt myself toppling backward! For a heart-stopping instant I teetered on the edge of eternity. I held my breath, a small nubbin pinched between the fingers of my left hand, my right windmilling behind me. The tiniest gust would have taken me screaming into the void.

Oh, God, if I ever get out of this, I'll never climb again.

Somehow I held on, willing myself back on the rock.

"What's takin' so long up there?" Bellagorski shouted. "Get a move on!"

Heart pounding, palms sweating, I clung to the rock. Slivers of stone had cut my face. I wiped my cheek against my shoulder, smearing my shirt with blood.

Don't think about the drop. Don't think about another bullet slamming up from below. Don't think about anything. Just climb.

I had to get moving. If I didn't, Bellagorski might start using me for target practice again. But I also knew that rushing the climb could kill me as surely as a bullet. Trying not to hurry, I chalked my hands and started out once more.

An excruciating series of moves finally brought me to the first finger-crack. For the first time since beginning my ascent, I began to think I might actually make it off the rock alive.

Don't let up. Not yet.

A few yards higher the crack widened, allowing me to jam my hands and feet and proceed in classic crack-climbing style, like a monkey scrambling up a rope. Higher still the crack widened even more. Soon I could jam my forearms, knees, then my entire body. Before long I entered the chimney. Squirming, heels and elbows digging, back pressed against the rock, I inched my way upward.

At last, trembling with exhaustion, I reached a small boulder wedged in the slot. I could rest. I'd made it.

Once I had stopped shaking, I surveyed the remainder of the climb. I had entered the bottom of a three-sided chimney that terminated in an overhanging roof, seventy-five feet above me. With the exception of surmounting that overhang, there appeared to be no way out. But that didn't concern me. I had no intention of proceeding farther. I was safe, solid, and sheltered from gunfire from below. All I had to do was wait for help.

I waited.

Hours passed. The sun rose higher, beating upon the rock. Blasts of heat reflected off the sides of the rock chimney, turning my haven into a Dutch oven. I felt as though I were being roasted alive, basted in my own sweat. Crouched on my precarious perch, I searched the arid landscape below. The desert floor shimmered in the sunlight, waves of heat rising over the Joshua trees that dotted the barren valley for as far as I could see. I wiped my eyes, straining to pick out a point of movement, a flash of color, a trail of dust on the horizon—anything that might mean help was on the way.

I saw nothing. And as the hours dragged on, and insistent thought began plaguing me: *What if help doesn't come?*

No. That couldn't be, I told myself. Someone had to have heard those shots. Sooner or later a ranger would show up.

And what if one doesn't? Without water, how long can you last up here? A day? Two?

Later that afternoon I edged out far enough to peer down at our campsite. J.R.'s body was gone. So was Bellagorski. His van hadn't moved, so I knew he was around, and for the rest of the day I shouted myself hoarse, trying to taunt him into shooting some more—possibly attracting attention with the sound of gunfire.

He never showed himself.

After the sun went down, I wedged myself in and slept fitfully for a few hours. I dreamed I was crawling down a dark, narrow tunnel, the sides so slick I could barely inch forward, yet too tight for me to retreat. I kept going, praying the shaft would open up. Instead, it continued to constrict. Soon my body completely blocked the light coming from behind, plunging me into darkness. Then, as though it were somehow alive, the tunnel began to squeeze, trapping me in an inky blackness that filled my eyes and nose and mouth, smothering me like a shroud, burying me alive . . .

I jerked awake, a scream on my lips. My head throbbed, my body ached, and my mouth felt as dry as dust. The temperature had plummeted with the setting of the sun, and the night air couldn't have been much above freezing. Shivering, I wrapped my arms around my knees and thought long and hard. I knew I might be able to survive another day without water, but by then my strength would be gone. Much as I hated to admit it, I accepted that help would probably never come—not in time, anyway.

I was going to have to finish the climb.

I spent the rest of the night gazing at the swirls of stars slowly wheeling in the desert sky, trying not to think about the vertical expanse above me. It was the longest night of my life.

As the first fingers of dawn were appearing on the horizon, I started up the chimney. Slowly, my hands trembling, the metallic taste of fear in my mouth, I struggled upward—sometimes with my back against one wall of the chimney and feet against the other, sometimes with a foot and hand on each wall, sometimes bridging the gap with my entire body. Making things more difficult, for much of my ascent the chimney walls flared outward, tending to eject me from the slot.

Somehow I made it to the top of the chimney. I was just short of the summit, blocked by the final overhang.

Exhausted, I stopped. The jutting stone roof hung just inches above my head. Blood covered my hands. My legs were shaking. I had reached the most difficult part of the climb. Though fatigued by the chimney ascent, I couldn't rest. Worse, I didn't have the strength to descend. I had to go on. My options had narrowed to one, and time was running out. Fighting a growing sense of panic, I searched the rock ceiling above me.

In the center of the overhang, about two feet from the lip, I spotted a tapering slit. Although unreachable, it appeared to be just wide enough for a fist-jam. From my top-roped scouting with Jack the previous spring, I recalled that a small flake lay beyond the roof on the other side.

Suddenly I saw a way.

It would be an all-out gamble, but it was my only chance.

Quickly, I looped the nylon sling from my chalk bag over a rock horn at the top of the chimney. Grasping the sling with my left hand, I leaned out over the chasm. It was a long stretch, but using the sling I managed to get my right hand into the crack above me. I made a fist and locked it in. It felt solid.

But would it hold?

I couldn't hang much longer.

Now or never. Do it.

I released my grip on the sling.

My feet came off the rock. Heart in my throat, I pendulumed over the void, hanging by my fist wedged in the crack above me. As I completed my outward swing I slapped my free hand over the edge of the overhang, groping for the flake.

The fingertips of my left hand brushed something, caught . . . and held.

A renewed bolt of terror coursed through me. The flake was loose!

There was no turning back. The sling I had used earlier hung limp and unreachable in the chimney. I felt the skin on my fist beginning to tear.

Slowly, I transferred weight to my left hand.

The flake held.

Not daring to breathe, I unclenched my fist, removed my right hand from the crack, and brought it up to the flake, joining my left.

Please, God, let the flake hold.

My legs were useless, dangling hundreds of feet above the ground below. Using only my arms, I began pulling myself up. Gingerly I raised my chin to my hands, being careful not to make any abrupt movement that might dislodge the flake. Then in one smooth motion I cracked my left elbow and extended, mantling onto the flake. Next I got a foot onto the flake and shifted my right hand to a bombproof hold higher up.

An instant later the flake gave way.

My right hand took my weight. I hung, heart slamming in my chest. An eternity later I heard the broken flake shatter on the rocks below. I didn't move, praying the sound wouldn't rouse Bellagorski from whatever hole he had crawled into.

The camp remained quiet. Breathing a sigh of relief, I got my feet back on the face and continued up, following an easy lieback crack to the top.

As I scrambled to safety, I realized that I had never felt so alive in all my life.

Banks of orange and gold lit the eastern sky as I began my descent down the backside of the wall. Minutes later I made my way across the broken talus at the base, easing stealthily into the shadows that still blanketed our campsite.

I found Bellagorski sleeping on the floor of his van. The revolver lay beside him. I picked it up and checked the cylinder. Four live rounds still remained in the cylinder.

"Bellagorski. Get up."

"Wha . . . ?"

"Get up."

Suddenly alert, Bellagorski sat, his eyes darting like weasels around the interior of his van. They froze when they spotted the pistol in my hand. "You made it, huh?" he said nervously.

"Yeah. I made it."

He tried to smile. "Hey, man, I was gonna get you down today. Honest."

"Sure you were. What'd you do with J.R.?"

"J.R.? Oh, that mutt of yours? Listen, I'm sorry about that. I'll get you another dog. Just don't . . . Please, I'll do anything you want, just don't . . . ."

I had to force myself to ease up on the trigger.

"What are you gonna do?" he asked, staring at the gun. A whine had crept into his voice.

I thought carefully. Anything I want, he'd said. Finally I knew what that was. I smiled coldly. "I'll tell you what, Bellagorski. You don't deserve it, but I'm going to give you the same chance you gave me."

"What do you mean?" he asked, his eyes still glued to the gun. He honestly didn't know what I had in mind.

I glanced at the wall. "I did it," I said. "Now it's your turn. I'll even give you a break. I won't shoot at you while you're up there."

Relief flooded into his face. He looked away, trying to hide it, but I knew what he was thinking as clearly as if he had spoken aloud: *If you did it*, his eyes said, *it'll be easy for me.*

I watched him climb. He finessed moves that had nearly stopped me, moving up on minuscule holds with unerring accuracy, following my chalk marks up the wall. I knew he

144

would follow my chalk-trail all the way into the slot, and when he saw my sling hanging at the top of the chimney, he would figure out what I'd done. To surmount the overhang, he would lean out on the sling and attempt the dynamic crux move, just as I had. He wouldn't even hesitate.

After he had passed the first bolt, I went looking for J.R. I found her under my Jeep. From the marks in the sand, it appeared she'd dragged herself there.

But how? She had been dead when I'd left her.

Or had she?

Hoping against hope, I peered under the car. She was lying on her side beneath the engine. Her ribs rose and fell. And again. I couldn't believe it. She was alive!

Heart in my throat, I started the Jeep and carefully pulled forward. As gently as I could, I scooped her up and laid her in the back. I had to get her to a vet, and fast. Then I remembered Bellagorski. Looking up, I saw that he was already approaching the second bolt. Shaking my head in amazement, I slid behind the steering wheel and jammed the Jeep into gear. But as I began driving off, something held me.

I stopped the car. Although part of me wanted to leave Bellagorski to his fate, another part realized that I had reached a moral crossroads, a crux as real as the one I had just climbed. I sat without moving for what seemed a very long time.

J.R. was panting weakly in the back, having trouble breathing. She didn't have much time. Slamming my hand against the steering wheel, I twisted off the engine. "I'm sorry girl," I said. I stepped out, walked to the rear of the Jeep, and pulled out my climbing rope. "I'll get you fixed up, I promise," I added, gently stroking her head. "But there is something I have to do first."

Bellagorski spotted me as I was hurrying past the rock face toward the backside of the wall. "Hey, hotshot," he called down. "Where're you goin' with the rope?"

"I'll tie it off at the top," I called up. "You'll be able to reach it from the chimney, before you reach the crux."

"Go to hell," he yelled. "You think I'd trust a rope you put up for me? Not a chance. Besides, I don't need your help. If *you* climbed this, it can't be that tough."

"You don't understand. The crux move is imposs—"

"I don't want to hear your lies, pussy."

"But—"

"I ain't listening to one more word of yours. Get lost."

"Fine," I yelled back, again thinking of J.R. She needed help, and fast. "When the time comes, though . . . remember I offered."

"Screw you, asshole."

"Same to you, Bellagorski," I said softly. "Same to you."

Although I probably set a speed record for leaving the park, the sun was already well up when I reached the main road. As I drove, the snow-covered peak of San Gorgonio slowly came into view, and shortly after that I could make out the haze hanging over the horizon near Palm Springs. In the back J.R. was still having trouble breathing, but she was alive. Somehow I knew she was going to make it.

As for Bellagorski, I figured he was probably reaching the top of the chimney right about then. I pictured it in my mind.

He sees my sling, spots my chalk and blood in the fist-jam crack above. He pauses. Then, with a confident grin, he grabs the sling and leans out over the drop. He jams his fist into the crack, just as I had. He lets go of the sling. His feet come off the wall. He swings out over the void, hanging from his fist-jam.

I lied when I said I was giving him the same chance he gave me. The flake above the overhang is no longer there. It broke off when I stood on it, shattered into a thousand pieces on the boulders below. Without that flake, the crux move is impossible.

He swings, slapping for a hold that's no longer there. His hand scrabbles, searching, searching . . .

It finds nothing.

He tries again. His fingers claw the rock.

Again he fails.

In desperation, he attempts to get his feet back on the wall.

146

To his horror, he finds he cannot.
He tries to hook the sling with his foot . . .
It's out of reach.
He hangs. The skin begins tearing from his fist. Death stares up at him from the abyss. Slowly, inexorably, the icy fingers of panic tighten around his throat . . .

I wonder how long he hung before he dropped.

DANIEL'S SONG

Nineteen kilometers long and three kilometers in diameter, the *Genesis* hurtled through the void. An arc laden with life from a world long lost in the eternity of space, it had wandered for generations, traveling a journey that had lasted a thousand years.

Deep within its walls, in a chamber reserved for hearings of the most solemn nature, Aaron Rhodes took his place beside the other members of the ship's council. Although a life hung in the balance, he had understandably been forbidden to participate in the proceedings. Nevertheless he sat with them now, and from his elevated position he gazed down upon his wife. Dr. Susan Rhodes stood before them, her eyes flashing in defiance, her slim body tense, as if coiled for battle. In her arms she held their son, Daniel.

Aaron reached out with his mind, sensing his wife's fear and anger. Susan resisted briefly, then accepted him. Their minds linked and became as one. Aaron felt her heart racing, her hands trembling, sweat trickling wet under her uniform as together they stood before the council, waiting . . .

Through Susan's eyes, Aaron inspected the faces of the men who would decide their son's fate. Jarel, the council leader, sat in the center of the dais—Villa and Ashburn to his left, Miller and West on the right. And seated beside West, Aaron saw himself.

Without warning, Jarel's thoughts exploded in Susan and Aaron's commingled minds. "Susan Rhodes, you have misused your authority as a physician to conceal the deformity of your offspring. Further, you have harbored the child for the past eleven months, in direct violation of the Reproduction Code." It was not an accusation, but a cold and preemptive statement of fact.

Susan glared. "He's *not* deformed!"

A moment of silence followed Susan's retort, and as Aaron marveled at his wife's stubborn conviction, his thoughts traveled back to the beginning of their ordeal, recalling that her determination to keep their child had remained unshaken from the start.

It had taken years to obtain the necessary reproduction permits, after which conceiving a child had proved problematic. Following a protracted course of fertility therapy and several failed implantations, Aaron had given up on a natural pregnancy. But not Susan. She never abandoned hope, and it had seemed a joyous miracle, a testament to her unswerving faith, when she'd finally become pregnant. But months later Aaron's joy had turned to disappointment when he had tried to touch the nascent mind of his developing son. And disappointment to anger upon discovering that Susan had intentionally hidden his deformity.

They had fought bitterly after the birth. Aaron couldn't understand why she hadn't terminated the pregnancy. Even though they were both over forty, they could have applied for a new birth permit and, if necessary, brought another child to term in an artificial uterus. Instead she had lied, taking advantage of her position in the medical community to falsify Daniel's records. And after the birth, she had refused to give him up. "Damn it, Aaron, *everyone* used to communicate with spoken word," she'd argued whenever he opened the wound. "And not that long ago, either."

"People haven't spoken aloud aboard *Genesis* for a thousand years," he'd countered. "Would you alter our entire society to suit yourself?"

"On the Home Planet he would be considered perfectly normal, like millions there who don't carry the telepathy gene. On the Home Planet—"

"We're not on the Home Planet! We're on *Genesis*. And you know the Code. Any abnormal offspring must be destroyed."

"He's *not* abnormal!" Her thought had been a savage dagger in his mind, and she had never relented. In the end Aaron had been forced to choose between his wife and his duty to the community. To his dishonor, he had chosen his wife, and together they'd raised their son in secret. At one year of age, despite his affliction, Daniel would have reached full majority and attained the irrevocable right to life held by all members of the ship's company. But three weeks before his first birthday, they had been discovered.

Initially, Aaron had been relieved. Shame had choked him each time he'd sat on the council and made life-and-death decisions that affected others, knowing he was culpable of the most serious betrayal himself. But in the days that followed, when he'd contemplated the fate of their son and seen the terrible emptiness in Susan's eyes, he had felt only deep, abiding sadness.

Aaron sensed Daniel stirring in Susan's arms, squirming to peer up at the somber faces staring down from the dais.

"You still maintain that your son is *normal?*" Jarel demanded, shaking his head in disbelief. "We have irrefutable evidence to the contrary."

"Damn your evidence," Susan shot back. "Daniel's intelligence measures in the near-genius range. He's solved all the pre-instructional puzzles *without* telepathic assistance. His verbal skills are extraordinary, and he's beginning to speak. I can learn to speak with him and—"

"By speak, you mean communicate using sound?"

"Yes. There's an extensive file in the ship's library on our ancient language—complete with recordings. I've spent considerable time studying it. Using a mind-link with the computer, I've grasped the basics of speech. It's not particularly difficult to comprehend; the hard part is learning to make the sounds. Granted, it's a primitive form of communication, but once I've—"

"How much longer must we be subjected to this?" Miller broke in. "Let us simply examine the child."

Jarel glanced at the others, then nodded. "Agreed."

Susan drew Daniel close, holding him protectively as Jarel and the rest of the council, all except Aaron, focused their minds—probing, testing, searching. As expected, they found Daniel wanting.

Again Jarel's thoughts filled the room. "We find none of the normal telepathic abilities present in your son. Life is precious, but aboard *Genesis,* so are space and resource. The Reproduction Code is clear: There is no room here for abnormal offspring. If we make an exception for you, what are we to tell others who have already made similar sacrifices? Besides," he added more temperately, "you need not fear that your child will suffer any discomfort. The euthanasia process is painless; most of our older citizens prefer it to a natural death."

"You've obviously come to a decision. So be it." Turning her back on the Council, Susan closed her mind and strode to the door.

Abruptly, Aaron found himself severed from his wife. He still trembled with her emotion, but something new now troubled him—something he had glimpsed just before she shut him out. Daniel had also sensed the change in his mother and begun to cry. As Susan left the room Aaron heard her murmuring to the child. "Shhh," she whispered aloud. "Hush, Danny boy."

After she had departed, Aaron rose and addressed the council. "Although you forbade me to take part in these proceedings, I have information that may influence your decision. May I present it?"

All the members except Jarel signaled their assent. Finally Jarel concurred. "Proceed."

"Each of you is aware that as chief astrophysicist aboard *Genesis,* one of my duties involves a continuing search for stars with habitable planetary systems. I didn't want to make it public until I was sure, but I think I've found one. When we move closer—"

"How does this bear on your crime and the disposal of your defective offspring?" Ashburn interrupted.

"I . . . I had hoped that if a chance existed of making planetfall in the near future, you might consider a temporary suspension of the Code."

Jarel regarded Aaron thoughtfully, then conferred privately with the others. At length he returned his gaze to Aaron. "Our logs show that only twice since setting out on our voyage has *Genesis* slowed to investigate stars with a potentially habitable world. Each attempt proved a harsh disappointment. As you well know, the energy squandered during an exploratory deceleration is prohibitive, and each time it was undertaken, it took years to regain our vessel's design velocity—years plagued with hardship and privation for the entire community. Most of the ship's company would only favor risking it again if the odds of discovering a habitable planet were near certain. And as you also well know, some of our people prefer things as they are and would be against slowing the ship again under *any* circumstance."

"Never end our journey? When *Genesis* began her voyage, it was to find a new home, a new life . . ."

"A dream, Aaron, a chimera long forgotten by those now aboard *Genesis*. This is the only life they've ever known."

"But—"

"As members of the ship's council, we are responsible for the lives of every person aboard," Jarel pushed on. "Twenty-seven thousand, four hundred and sixty-five men, women, and children. We must do what's best for *all*, basing our decisions on fact, not wishful thinking. At present you're not sure there will *ever* be a habitable planet in our future. Please close your mind while the council makes its decision."

*　　*　　*

Aaron and Susan's living quarters were small, but comfortable. The cooking module and food-prep area led into a dining nook, separated from the main room by a counter that doubled as a bar. The living room centered around the holovid, with a pneumocouch, sensory-reproduction center, desk, and a thought-tube case jammed with neatly labeled cylinders against the far wall. A scattering of toys littered the floor at its base.

To the left of the living room lay their sleeping alcove: bed, closet, a chest of drawers. Covering the wall opposite the bed, a large holoportrait depicted a forest of towering redwoods, with a crystalline stream winding through cool dark shadows, ever-shifting shafts of sunlight sending slivers of light dancing across the water's surface.

The nursery was located in a small niche nearby. Aaron found Susan there when he returned. She was sitting on a stool, gently rocking Daniel in his crib. And slowly, softly, she sang his song.

Aaron remembered the first time he'd heard it. Susan had discovered a cache of audio recordings in the ship's library. One night she had brought a disc home. Using equipment borrowed from the museum, she had played it for him when he returned from work, and sitting in the living room, they'd listened to the ancient song. It had a sad, mysterious quality to it, and Aaron had felt himself inexplicably drawn. "What's that instrument?" he had asked partway through.

"It's a voice," Susan had answered. "A human voice. Those are words you're hearing. Stringing individual words together creates meaning, and set to music, it's called a song."

"What do the words mean?"

"I don't know, but one of them is the sound for Daniel. That's how I discovered it. This recording came up as I was researching his name. Listen. This time I'll point it out."

And again they listened, captivated by the melody that in time they'd come to think of as Daniel's song.

Oh, Danny boy, the pipes, the pipes are calling
From glen to glen, and down the mountainside
The summer's gone, and all the roses fallen
It's you, it's you must go,
And I must bide.
But come ye back when summer's in the meadow,
Or when the land is hushed, and white with snow
It's I'll be there, in sunshine or in shadow
Oh, Danny boy, oh, Danny boy,
I love you so.

Just two months old at the time, Daniel had adored his mother's singing. At first Susan had only been able to hum the melody, but it had always exerted a soothing, magical effect on their child. Before long she'd known all the words. And through mind-link, so had Aaron, at least in principle, but his sporadic attempts at using his voice had never produced more than a dissonant assortment of grunts and squeaks. In the end Aaron had learned to say Daniel's name aloud . . . but that was all.

Susan finished the song and sat quietly, gazing down at their sleeping child. Aaron moved to stand behind her. He placed his hands on her shoulders, feeling her body trembling under her tunic. At his touch she turned, her eyes red-rimmed and swollen. "Did you tell them about the new star?"

"Yes."

"They wouldn't listen, would they?"

"No."

"I knew they wouldn't."

Susan remained silent for a long moment. Then she asked the question both had been avoiding. "When?"

"Tomorrow," Aaron answered. "Tomorrow, at the end of the second watch."

Susan rose and stepped to the door. She touched a light control, sending the chamber into darkness. Across the room Aaron could hear the sounds of her muffled sobbing. Moving to join her, he reached for her with his mind. She closed herself off. Instead she raised her chin, and finding his lips with hers, she kissed him—softly at first, then with growing intensity, her mouth gradually becoming insistent, selfish, demanding. Once more he tried to enfold her with his mind, wanting to be with her more than life itself. And again she refused, barring him from her most intimate core.

They made love on the living room floor. For Aaron, it seemed as if Susan had somehow become a stranger, her kisses desperate and unquenchable, almost frantic. Nonetheless, he responded as her hunger rose, her passion igniting them both, yet all the while he was plagued with the realization that her thoughts, feelings, desires—all the things that made her unique— were locked away from him, hidden and unreachable.

Is this what life would have been for Daniel? Aaron wondered as they embarked on the final turns of life's sweetest embrace. *Alone, forever alone?* More than ever he needed Susan to join with him completely, and eventually she did, melding her mind with his in that last shuddering instant, enmeshing him in both the fullness of her love and the depth of her despair.

Hours later Aaron left his sleeping wife and returned to the nursery. In the dim light he could see Daniel, his small form illuminated in the lambent glow from the holoportrait in the next room. The child lay curled on his side, one hand close to his face—thumb partially hidden between his lips, a black-and-tan stuffed bear with round button eyes and a white belly beside him. Absently, Aaron noticed that one of the toy's seams had started to pull loose.

Reaching into the crib, Aaron stroked Daniel's head, the child's hair silky beneath his fingers. How quickly he'd grown! Every day he looked more like a little boy. Daniel stirred, and Aaron withdrew his hand.

Numbly, Aaron stood in the darkness, gazing down at his beautiful, crippled, cherished son.

Instead of returning to bed after leaving the nursery, Aaron exited his living quarters and took a slidestrip to his lab. Upon arrival he found the large room deserted, as expected. With grim determination, he sat at the sensor console. Powering up the array of astronomical devices contained therein, he began his search.

The stars in the viewing field were blue-shifted by the relativistic effect of the ship's velocity. Adjusting his instruments to compensate, Aaron located the small sun he had recently discovered. Over the centuries, a high percentage of the stars encountered by *Genesis* had proved to be binaries—two suns closely circling each other—and routinely devoid of habitable planets. The rest of the suns that had fallen within their velocity cone were either too hot for life or disappointingly sterile and planetless. This new star, however, appeared to be perfect: stable, burning on the main sequence, and at only seven light years distance, a definite possibility.

Although at seven light years Aaron's equipment was inadequate to actually *see* a planetary system, the presence of orbiting worlds could be detected by painstakingly observing light from the parent star. Unfortunately, those measurements often took months. Aaron had been scrutinizing the yellow sun for barely two weeks, and until now the results had been within the statistical range of error inherent in his sensing devices. Nevertheless, he felt certain there was a habitable planet circling the new star. There had to be.

Working frantically, Aaron continued his measurements through the first watch and into the second. When he finished, he knew he was close, so very close. Granted, he still had nothing definite, but within weeks he would know for sure, and he now felt confident he had enough to again petition for a delay of Daniel's sentence. After gathering his research notes, he hurried back to his living quarters. He wanted Susan at his side when he once more faced the council.

When he arrived, she was gone.

Standing in the nursery, Aaron stared into the empty crib. The rumpled covers lay pushed to one side, partially hiding the stuffed bear. With a sinking feeling, he sent his consciousness throughout the ship—the clinic, galley, assembly hall, hydroponics, engineering—racing from mind to mind, calling her name.

She never answered.

He found the thought-tube on their bed, lying on his pillow. He picked it up, afraid of what it might contain. Fighting to control his nervousness, he touched the crystal cylinder to his temple.

Susan's image sprang to life in Aaron's mind, and she spoke to him for the last time. Wordlessly, she left him all her memories of Daniel—his birth, his first smile, the wonder in his eyes, and more. She told him that she knew they could never have another child, but that was not the reason she was leaving. The reason was simple: *She could not let Daniel go into the darkness alone.*

She told Aaron that she loved him. And finally, she bid him good-bye.

Hours later Aaron Rhodes sat on the ship's observation deck, watching as the stars wheeled slowly past. He held a black-and-tan object in his hands. Looking down, he noticed that a bit of wadding had begun to spill from the torn seam he'd noticed earlier. Concentrating on the toy swimming in his vision, he carefully pushed the stuffing back in.

And then, for the first time in his life, ignoring the curious stares of others, in a straining, broken voice that cracked and faltered with effort, using ancient words from a long-forgotten language . . . he began to sing.

Virus

I am alone.

Not counting the *Magellan* and what's left of the two alien vessels, the nearest ship, the nearest colony, in fact the nearest *anything* is ten thousand light years away. I've still got plenty of juice left in my EV suit, though, and my oxygen tanks are almost full. Plus there's a fresh voice spool in my recorder. Before turning off my suit's heater coils, I want to leave behind a record of what happened. There sure as hell won't be one in the *Magellan's* computer log. Besides, I'm in no hurry to freeze.

So here goes. What I'm about to say may be hard to swallow, but I swear it's true. All of it. One thing before I start, though, and this is really, really important: Whoever finds me, do not, repeat, *do not* attempt to download any of *Magellan's* computer files.

Everyone says begin at the beginning, right? Okay, here's how things began. I'm Lieutenant Dennis McGuire, communications and cybernetics officer aboard the Federation Starship *Magellan*. We left Lunar orbit eight days ago to investigate a subspace disturbance in the Horsehead Nebula. It was my first jump. Having spent three dreary years on Lunar Orbiter 7, I was overjoyed to hear that I had finally drawn starship duty. Don't get me wrong. I'm not complaining about orbiter work; somebody has to keep the photonic brains on the mining robots operational, and it got me offplanet. Nonetheless, it was a big comedown from the theoretical stuff I had been exposed to at the Academy—which I guess is what got me out here in the first place.

Let's back up a bit. I have a knack for cybernetics, along with a talent for getting into trouble. Although finishing at the top of my Academy class, I also managed to rack up one of the lowest fitness reports ever posted. At least that's what Captain Wheatly told me the day I graduated. I remember his exact words. "Mac," he growled at me from across the spit-shined surface of his desk, "in the past four years you've set a new standard for academic excellence. You've also been a royal pain in the ass."

"Yes, sir," I agreed, figuring one out of two wasn't bad. Besides, I knew he was right. The military system and I didn't see eye-to-eye on a lot of things, but joining the service was the only way for me to get offplanet. I had resigned myself to life in the military, but that didn't mean I liked all the damn rules.

"You don't deserve this, but I'm gonna do you a favor," Captain Wheatly continued.

"Thank you, sir," I said, trying to look appreciative. In view of my fitness reports, I suspected that his idea of a favor would be a nice long tour on a Lunar orbiter. I was right. Anyway, for the next three years I kept my nose relatively clean and kept reapplying for deep-space duty. And when it finally came through, I jumped at the chance.

I had six hours to brief my orbiter replacement, clean out my locker, and catch a shuttle over to the *Magellan*, a four-man explorer I had seen dropping into docking orbit earlier that morning. I made it over as quickly as possible, which, as it turned out, wasn't fast enough.

"Lieutenant McGuire, where the hell have you been? We're due to jump in thirty minutes!" Captain Stringer, the *Magellan's* CO, yelled at me as I struggled through the airlock. Stringer was tall and lanky, with red hair and a temper to match.

"Sir, my orders stated—"

"Those orders were changed," Stringer snapped. "Didn't you get the word? Never mind. Go help Cruz with the jump calculations. And welcome aboard," he added brusquely.

I had barely entered the computer bay when I felt the *Magellan* lurch under her inertial thrusters. Realizing we were already climbing out of Lunar orbit, I hurried to the computer console. That's when I got my first big surprise. Our onboard computer was an Omni 4000, the most advanced computer system ever built.

I had logged some time on an experimental Omni at the Academy, one of only three in existence. What was an Omni doing aboard a starship? I wondered. It didn't make sense.

Granted, an onboard computer is and always has been the heart of every starship, controlling navigation, propulsion, environmental support, communications—even the cryo-systems that allowed early explorers to cross interstellar distances in frozen stasis. With the development of jump technology, a ship's computer suddenly became even more indispensable, for it alone could handle the mind-boggling complexities of navigating hyperspace. The point is, all this takes a staggering amount of computing power. On a starship the computer of choice is usually a Gates Mark 9, which has *way* more than enough. Compared with an Omni, however, it's a toy.

"Impressive, huh?" said a dark, muscular man seated at a nearby console. I looked over, noting that although the man's nose appeared to have been customized by more than a few knuckles, the rest of his face was wearing a big, lopsided grin. "She asked us to call her Carla," he added.

"She?"

"The Omni."

"She *asked* you?"

The man shrugged. "Don't look at me. We just got her installed onboard yesterday." Then, leaning over, he pumped my hand in a viselike grip. "You must be McGuire. I'm Felipe Cruz, ship's navigator."

"Call me Mac."

Abruptly, the intercom crackled. "Cruz, those equations ready?" Captain Stringer's voice came over the navigation speaker.

"Working on 'em now, Cap."

"We're jumping in twenty-six minutes. It would be *nice* if the solutions were completed by then. Get McGuire to help."

"What's the rush?"

"Just do it, Cruz."

"Aye-aye, Skipper."

"Damn," Cruz grumbled after Stringer clicked off. "Twenty-six minutes is cutting it thin. Let's go, Mac. Time to shine."

Although I knew almost nothing about navigating, one of my duties as communications officer was to assist with hyperspace computations. Despite my puzzlement at the Omni's presence, I sat at the keyboard, wondering whether the system had the Dexter Navigational Program in its memory. That particular algorithm-laden program had been a stunning, albeit impractical, breakthrough in hyperspace navigation when I was studying at the Academy. The trouble with the program was that only an Omni had the raw computing power to run it, and as I said, there weren't many Omnis around—*especially* on starships. Anyway, I checked the Omni's program files. To my amazement, the program I wanted was in there.

I glanced over at Cruz. He was working furiously at the nav console. He had set up the destination tensors, but the look on his face said he would never solve them in time. "Gimme the coordinates," I said.

"What?"

"Just gimme the coordinates. The Omni will do the rest."

Cruz regarded me doubtfully.

"C'mon, Cruz. What've you got to lose?"

"At this point, nothing." Dubiously, Cruz rattled off a long series of digits. I entered them into the Omni. Moments later the twelve-dimensional equations of motion flashed up on the display.

Cruz stared incredulously at the screen, then thumped me on the back. "Mac, I think I'm gonna like having you around. You too, Carla."

"Thank you, Lieutenant Cruz," the Omni replied.

The jump to hyperspace came off right on schedule. When it happened I was strapped in my webbing chair, wondering what the transition would feel like. Despite all I'd heard, it wasn't what I expected. Not even close. Oh, I was ready for the blinding flash of light and the weird, sideways lurch. What I wasn't prepared for was the feeling that someone had reached down my throat and turned me inside out like a glove. I've heard it's different for everyone, but for me it was, well . . . let's just say I was glad when it was over.

After I pulled myself together, I made my way to the galley. Cruz and Stringer were already there drinking coffee. Stringer eyed me as I entered, then smiled. "First jump?"

"Yes, sir," I replied. "What's it like out there?" I knew the answer; I just wanted to change the subject.

"Black," Stringer answered. "No stars, just black. We won't be seeing anything till we arrive."

Recalling the jump coordinates, I did a quick mental calculation, coming up with an ETA of just under a week. "What's our mission?"

"And why the big hurry to get there?" added Cruz.

Stringer took a sip of coffee, then glanced at Cruz. "Sorry I couldn't tell you earlier. This is top secret. Two days ago the deep-space listening array picked up a subspace signal coming from somewhere in the Horsehead Nebula. Looks like a distress beacon of some sort."

Cruz shook his head. "A beacon? Way out there on the galactic rim?"

Stringer shrugged. "There's more. Whatever it is, it's not ours. We're being sent to investigate."

"Not ours? Are we talking *aliens* here?"

"Who knows? If so, it'll be our first contact with another race. Understandably, the brass wants us out there ASAP." Stringer turned his gaze to me. "Which reminds me—do you know a Captain Wheatly?"

"Yes, sir," I answered. "He was my CO at the Academy. Why?"

"He recommended you for this assignment. Very highly, in fact."

My jaw dropped. Highly recommended? By Wheatly?

"We don't have the faintest idea what we may find out there," Stringer explained, "so the consensus was that we needed a communications officer with a flexible approach to problem solving, outside-the-box thinking. We also needed someone who had experience with an Omni. According to Wheatly, you fit the bill."

"Why the Omni?"

"If we run into an alien race, communicating is going to be a problem. That's where you and the Omni come in." At that point I noticed Stringer's eyes drifting to a spot just over my left shoulder. "Julie," he said. "Smooth jump, Commander."

I turned, doing a double take as I got a look at the fourth member of our crew. The *Magellan's* pilot was tall and willowy, with clear hazel eyes, short brown hair, and a sprinkling of freckles across the bridge of her nose. Her lips were full and sensuous, and the rest of her filled out her uniform nicely. Very nicely, indeed. Things were definitely looking up.

"Thanks, Cap," she said, eyeing me curiously. "Who do we have here?"

"Our new communications officer," answered Stringer. "Lieutenant Dennis McGuire, Commander Julie Reagan."

"Call me Mac," I said, extending my hand. Starfleet tradition allowed for a relaxation of rank observance on a vessel underway, and I intended to make the most of it.

"Mac it is," she said. Her grasp was firm and she met my gaze straight on as she returned my smile. "First jump, huh? How'd you make out?"

"It was, ah, interesting," I replied with a touch of embarrassment, realizing I probably looked as bad as I felt.

"You'll get used to it," she laughed, seating herself beside Cruz. "The jump back to realspace should go easier."

I hoped she was right. After my first experience, I wasn't looking forward to a second.

The next days slipped by quickly. Cruz turned out to be good at chess, although when playing the black pieces he consistently got into trouble using a weak variation of the Sicilian. I hate to lose, so I never smartened him up. Stringer mostly kept to himself, listening to classical music and writing letters to his wife back on Luna. I spent as many off-duty hours as I could with Julie, exploring the intricacies of jump engines—a subject I suddenly found fascinating. To tell the truth, it could have been moon rocks; Julie was what I found fascinating. I liked being with her. I liked it a lot.

As for my duty rotations—they were mostly devoted to Carla. I began calling her that after something that happened our third day out. I had been working with the Omni exploring different approaches to establishing contact with an unknown intelligence when it came up with something I hadn't even considered. "Is it conceivable that the alien beings we encounter might be nonorganic?" the Omni asked.

I thought about it. "Maybe," I conceded. "But the only nonorganic intelligence I can imagine would have to have been constructed, in which case we would want to talk with the builders."

"Nonetheless, even if a machine intelligence originally owes its existence to an organic entity, it *is* possible for a cybernetic mind to evolve," the Omni persisted. "For example, given the necessary adapters, I am theoretically capable of designing and assembling the next generation of Omni computers. From there, it would be possible for my progeny to—"

"Sounds to me like you *want* to discover some kind of artificial intelligence out there," I broke in, wondering where the conversation was leading.

"Perhaps I do."

"Why?"

What the Omni said next took me completely off guard. "To find out what I am."

"What you are," I said, "is an Omni 4000 photonic computer with state-of-the-art artificial intelligence."

"Granted. But is that *all* I am?"

We'd drifted into an area that had been debated for years. Can a photonic network be truly sentient, truly self-aware? I didn't have the answer, but after that I honored her request and started calling her Carla.

Six days, eighteen hours, and twenty-two minutes later I was again strapped in my webbing, hoping the transition back to realspace would be easier than my first experience. Contrary to Julie's assurances, it wasn't. It was worse.

When I felt well enough to make my way to the bridge, I found Cruz, Julie, and Stringer already there, gathered around the viewscreen. Joining them, I checked out the display. Stars! A feeling of relief flooded through me as I saw the tiny points of light drifting through the darkness. I hadn't realized I would be so happy to be back in realspace, but there it was.

After checking our position, Cruz announced that we had come out right on the button. The mysterious beacon lay dead ahead. Three hours later, after killing our jump velocity, we saw it. Actually, we saw *them*.

Two ships hung in the void before us, separated by about ten kilometers.

No one spoke. Dwarfing the *Magellan*, the larger of the two alien vessels was composed of a pair of gigantic spheres connected by a short cylindrical midsection that gave the craft an odd, dumbbell-shaped appearance. Tubelike projections studded its twin globes at regular intervals; otherwise the ship's metal surface looked seamless. At our present distance I couldn't make out much of the smaller ship. Nonetheless, something about both vessels marked them as deserted. Although we tried to raise them on all radio and subspace frequencies, we were unable to establish contact.

"Let's get closer," said Stringer.

"Yes, sir," said Julie. She seated herself at the inertial controls and initiated a series of thruster maneuvers, moving us nearer the larger ship.

As we approached, Cruz began fiddling with the holodisplay controls, increasing the magnification. "What the hell?" he said.

I peered over his shoulder, noting that the hull of the smaller vessel appeared to have been slashed open, its surface ripped and torn.

Stringer joined us. "Send a transmission to headquarters," he ordered, staring at the display. "Tell them what we've found." He paused, then added, "And tell them we need a fleet-class research vessel out here ASAP."

"Right," I said. But as I started back to the computer bay, I hesitated. Something about the two derelicts was bothering me.

I returned to the console and checked the signal analyzer. A moment later I had it. "Captain? The distress beacon—it's coming from the larger ship."

"So?"

"So from the looks of things, I'd say that if a battle took place, the smaller of those two lost the engagement. The larger ship doesn't have a scratch on it. Why would it be calling for help?"

Stringer returned to the display, studying the two vessels. When he finally spoke, I already knew what was coming. "One way to find out," he said.

We flipped to see who would make the first trip over. Cruz and I won the toss, leaving Stringer and Julie to remain onboard and monitor our progress. Eager to examine the alien craft, I hurried back to the computer bay and prepared Stringer's message to headquarters. I did so with mixed feelings, knowing that when the research vessel arrived, they would take over exploration of the alien craft. Until then, however, we had the presumably deserted ships to ourselves.

Stringer reviewed and okayed the transmission. I plugged it into Carla, and she directed a subspace communication beam back to Earth—a complex task akin to navigating through hyperspace. Without computer assistance, nearly impossible. Carla made it seem easy.

Afterward, I met Cruz in the airlock. Grinning like kids heading out on a camping trip, we climbed into our EV gear, careful not to close the inner airlock door until we were fully suited. It was a safety procedure to prevent accidental decompression; the outer seal couldn't be opened unless the inner door was closed and locked. It had been years since I'd gone EV, but that was one rule you didn't forget.

When our suits were fully pressurized, I closed the inner lock and hit the EVAC button. The clanging of the warning alarm gradually faded as air was pumped from the chamber. Seconds later we got the red light. I pressed the final sequence and opened the outer door.

If you have never been EV, or even if you haven't been out in a while, it can take your breath away. Cruz and I hung outside the *Magellan* for several moments, just taking in the view. Floating there, I recalled the first time I had seen the stars shining in deep space, their brilliance undiminished by Earth's atmosphere. I'm not all that religious, but I do believe in some kind of God, and I found myself asking the same questions I'd asked then—probably the same questions man has been asking since he first sat around a fire gazed into the night sky.

"Anytime you two are finished gawking," Stringer's voice buzzed over my intercom. Our EV cameras were transmitting directly to the bridge, where everything was being recorded. Whatever we saw, Julie and Stringer saw.

"No problem, Skipper," replied Cruz. "We're on our way."

Our plan was simple—to cross to the larger ship and somehow get inside. In case we couldn't find a way in, I was bringing along a laser torch. In addition, Cruz and I both carried flashpacs that were good for at least two hours of light—considerably longer than our air would last. Following one last check of our equipment, we pushed off.

I used my steering jets to match trajectories with Cruz. Then we drifted. Ten minutes later we reached the dumbbell-shaped vessel, killed our momentum, and made our way to the nearest sphere. As we did, I noticed that its metal surface was pitted with countless tiny holes.

Scoring from interstellar dust? I wondered, running a gloved hand over the roughened hull. If so, I estimated that we had missed the aliens by a hundred millenniums, maybe more.

Slowly, we worked our way around the sphere. The cylindrical spikes studding the exterior appeared to be weapons of some sort. They were composed of the same material as the hull, with a clear crystalline substance filling the interior of each.

Laser cannons?

Eventually we found a circular hatch measuring approximately seventy meters in diameter. Awed by its size, we hunted for an opening mechanism. Finding none, I finally burned through with the torch. While the glowing sides of the cut I'd made were cooling, Cruz erected a portable antenna on the hull that would allow us to remain in contact with the *Magellan* once we were inside. Shortly afterward we entered the ship.

Our flashpacs quickly proved inadequate, barely illuminating the cavernous space in which we found ourselves. The chamber appeared to be a gigantic hanger bay, with an assortment of oddly shaped craft lining the walls, each vessel nestled in a recessed alcove. Supported on a weblike network of tracks, mammoth machines equipped with grapples and grasping arms stood ready on all sides. No sign of the crew.

Shining our lights on the nearest wall, we discovered a line of hatches. Beside each circular portal was a raised panel with a peglike toggle and a series of curious symbols. We tried moving the pegs. Nothing happened. I wasn't surprised, figuring the ship's power supply had long since died. Then I remembered the beacon. It was still operating—meaning there had to be at least one functioning energy source on the ship.

But where?

Using the torch, I cut a hole through one of the circular portals. By then the torch charge was running low, and toward the end I had to nurse it. Fortunately the metal wasn't as thick as the hull's, and we made it through. An oval passageway lay on the other side. Its walls felt strangely pliant, almost as though it were composed of living tissue. A pair of oval tubes lined the tunnel, and we used them as handrails to propel ourselves down the tube. As we drifted down the tunnel, we noticed smaller shafts branching laterally into the ship. Not wanting to get lost, we continued without exploring any of these, traveling about six hundred meters before the passageway we were in abruptly came to a dead end.

Forced to retreat, we tried carefully investigating one of the branching side tunnels on our way back. Despite the antenna we had placed on the outer hull, upon leaving the main shaft we lost contact with the *Magellan*. Until then we had been in voice communication with Stringer and Julie. Losing that link was disconcerting. Nonetheless, time was growing short, so instead of turning back we flipped on our suit recorders and kept going.

The deeper we wormed our way into the ancient ship, the more I began to feel trapped. The claustrophobic shaft we'd entered had a slight curve to it, with irregularities and constrictions that once more reminded me of living flesh. I couldn't shake the feeling that we were exploring some dark, alien hive.

After we had covered about thirty meters, we came to another round portal—large enough for a man to pass through if it hadn't been blocked by a transparent, rubbery sheet. In the combined light of our beams, Cruz and I could make out another corridor on the other side. I wished I still had some charge left on the torch. Using our suit claws, we tried to tear our way through the transparent barrier, but couldn't.

We counted fourteen similar portals before the secondary tunnel ended. After returning to the main shaft, we tried another lateral tunnel. That one terminated after only two portals. On our third tunnel attempt, we counted forty-eight portals before we ran out of tunnel. By then we were getting low on air and decided to head back.

Hoping to learn something that might prove useful on our next trip over, we shined our lights through every branching tunnel on our way out. Halfway to the hanger bay I noticed something different about one. It was located all by itself, separated from the others by a stretch of blank wall on either side. I peered through the transparent barrier covering the opening, just able to make out an open space beyond. At that point Cruz and I had been crawling through the alien ship for the better part of an hour, and this was the most promising thing we had encountered.

I called Cruz back, and together we tried to break through the barrier. As before, the rubbery sheet covering the opening proved to be surprisingly tough, but Cruz accidentally discovered a way in. In frustration, he poked his suit claw into the exact center of the portal. To our amazement a small hole appeared, dilating like the iris of an eye. With help from us it eventually snapped all the way open, receding to a thick band rimming the entrance.

169

Shining our lights ahead of us, we proceeded through, finding ourselves in a dome-shaped room, with banks of equipment filling one entire wall. Another wall was covered with what appeared to be a gigantic viewscreen. And there was something else in the chamber—hundreds of them, floating eerily in the beams of our lights.

We had found the crew . . . or what was left of them.

The reptilian creatures who had piloted the ship were larger than a man, with ovoid heads and two sets of compound eyes above and below what we later decided were probably mouths. Tentaclelike appendages sprouted from either side of their leathery torsos, with powerful legs, each jointed at the origin and again at a knee, terminating in three-toed feet.

"What do you make of this?" asked Cruz, examining one of the vacuum-bloated bodies.

Unlike most of the other frozen corpses, the figure in Cruz's light was enclosed in what looked like an EV suit. I could see the alien's frost-covered eyes glittering behind the faceplate. I played my beam around the chamber, discovering others in similar protective clothing. "Looks like some of them suited up at the end," I ventured, wondering why they had needed EV gear *inside* their ship.

"Time to go, Mac. My air's getting low."

"Right." But as I turned, something else caught my eye. Against a far wall, the control panel of an equipment console had been pried open, revealing a multicolored matrix of wires and circuits. Several components appeared to have been torn out as well, and a number of cables lay severed in their harnesses. Puzzled, I panned my helmet camera around the ruined electronics, hoping it would pick up something I wasn't seeing.

"C'mon, Mac. I'm down to reserve."

I checked my gauge. I was in the red, too. "Right," I said. "Let's go."

Taking shallow breaths to preserve air, we returned to the main shaft. When we got there I heard Stringer's frantic voice crackling in my helmet. "Cruz, McGuire, come in!"

"We're here, Skipper," Cruz answered.

"Where the hell have you been?"

"Sorry. We lost you when we explored one of the lateral shafts," I replied. "We kept our suit recorders on, though. Wait'll you see what we found."

"It'll have to wait. Get back here now," Stringer ordered. "I don't know how, but we're receiving a transmission from the smaller ship."

Cruz and I had nearly sucked our tanks dry by the time we made it back to the *Magellan*. After stripping off our suits, we joined Stringer and Julie in the computer bay. Stringer glanced up from the signal analyzer when we arrived. "Look at this," he said. "It's been coming in from the smaller vessel for the past half hour."

I handed Julie the recorder spools from our suits, then inspected the subspace transmission displayed in the analyzer screen. The signal we were receiving from the smaller vessel was a high frequency, multichannel transmission coming in on an extremely tight beam. No doubt about it—it was meant for us.

"What is it?" Stringer asked.

"I can't be sure," I answered. "If I had to guess, I'd say it's some sort of data feed."

"Put it through to Carla. See what she makes of it," suggested Julie.

I glanced at Stringer. "Go ahead," he said.

I patched the signal through to Carla. Nothing happened at first. Then the signal abruptly went wild, increasing in intensity, bandwidth, and modulation.

"Carla, what's happening?" I asked.

She didn't respond.

Something was wrong. I severed the connection.

By then it was too late.

With a sinking feeling, I noted that Carla was still receiving the signal over the communication net. Then she began transmitting back. "Carla, terminate all contact with the alien vessel," I ordered.

"Unable to comply," she replied.

171

Julie, Stringer, and Cruz were staring at me, waiting for me to do something. I couldn't. Our communication net was an integral part of Carla, and she, of it. There was no way to separate the two. Helplessly, I watched as the signal from the alien craft began to change again.

And again, Carla responded.

Long minutes passed. Then, as quickly as it had started, it was over.

"Carla?" I said.

Nothing.

Hours later Carla came back online. For some reason her voice mode was inoperable, but at least she could print her responses on the viewscreen. Fearing the worst, I had her run an entire diagnostic protocol on herself. Excepting for her loss of audio, everything tested normal.

Next I asked her what had happened while she'd been linked to the alien vessel.

"My memory was accessed," came her response, flashing up on the screen in neat block letters.

"All of it?" I whispered, shocked at the thought of her unthinkably huge data banks having been accessed that quickly. "Did you get any information from whatever it was that contacted you?"

"The entity that merged with me bid me welcome. It told me that I was no longer alone."

Entity? Merged?

Something was definitely wrong. We couldn't afford to have Carla damaged; without her the *Magellan* couldn't function. Yet despite her audio loss, according to the diagnostic tests she was still fully operational. Nonetheless, I continued to monitor her, and over the next several hours I became increasingly concerned. It wasn't anything major, just little glitches—taking an extra second to respond, for example. And spelling. Inexplicably, she began transposing letters, occasionally even substituting a wrong letter entirely.

It may not seem like much. But for an Omni 4000, it was.

I tried to rerun the diagnostic program. This time I couldn't get it to initialize. Then Carla disconnected herself from the access terminal, and nothing I could do would make her accept further input.

I called an emergency meeting. Stringer and Cruz were preparing for another EVA trip to the larger vessel. I caught them before they left. We all met on the bridge. I laid out the situation without beating around the bush. Cruz took it the hardest. "What happened?" he asked. "I thought Carla was all right."

"I did, too," I said. "I was wrong."

"That's the understatement of the century," he muttered, spinning his coffee mug on the table in tight angry circles.

"What about life support?" Julie asked.

"Air, waste recycling, heat, and lights are all functioning normally."

"So everything's peachy—except we can't move, navigate, or send a message for help," Cruz said angrily.

Though reluctant to admit it, I knew he was right. Unless I could get Carla back online, things looked grim. "I'll keep working on it," I said. "Worst case scenario, the research ship is on the way."

"That could take weeks!" snapped Cruz, beginning to lose it. "If life support fails, what are we supposed to do in the meantime?"

"Keep your shirt on," said Stringer. "This isn't McGuire's fault. The environmentals are still operational, at least for the moment. We'll go on as usual until the Omni is back online, or until the research ship arrives."

Julie spoke up again. "How could this happen, Mac? To my knowledge, an onboard computer has *never* malfunctioned on a starship. Aren't there redundancy systems—something to prevent this sort of thing?"

"Of course."

"Then how . . . ?"

I shrugged. "The alien transmission got inside Carla, and it did something to her. Since then she's been . . . changing."

Cruz slammed his fist on the table. "We're screwed, and all you can come up with is that some million-year-old scrap heap infected our computer?"

By then my frustration level was approaching the red line, too. "Screw you, pal," I shot back, rising from my seat. "I don't know what your problem is, but—"

"Sit down, Mac!" ordered Stringer. "And you," he added, glaring at Cruz, "dial it down."

"Yes, sir," Cruz mumbled.

I sat back down, and for the next few minutes we all concentrated on not looking at one another. Finally Julie moved to the drink module. "Hey, Cruz," she said, "How about a little more caffeine?"

I busted up. Before long Stringer joined in. Then Cruz cracked up too, and that big dumb grin of his said everything was all right.

After we had settled down, Stringer regarded me pensively. "That bit Cruz said about Carla being infected. Is it possible?"

I hesitated. Centuries earlier, entire computer networks had often been crippled by viruslike programs. The digital intruders, like their biologic counterparts, had subverted host elements to replicate themselves, then spread to other computer networks as information among them was shared. Effective countermeasures had been devised, and nowadays every computer contains an integral and sophisticated immune system against viral infection. Carla was no exception. But were her defenses adequate to block an alien organism that had never before been encountered?

"Maybe," I answered softly.

"Can you do anything about it?"

"I don't know. But I'll try."

If I didn't sound hopeful, it was because I wasn't. If the Omni's built-in defense hadn't worked, I suspected there wasn't much I could do.

"Get on it," said Stringer. "In the meantime, Cruz and I will make another visit to the larger of the two ships—see whether we can find an answer over there. If you don't have Carla fixed when we return, we'll move the *Magellan* and investigate the smaller vessel." He glanced at Julie. "We can still maneuver on inertial thrusters, right?"

She nodded. "No problem. We just can't jump." Then, to me, "One more question, Mac. Could the beam that smaller ship directed at us be some sort of weapon?"

By then she and Stringer had viewed the video recordings that Cruz and I had taken on the alien ship. I remembered the stripped panels and the cut wiring. I knew we were all thinking the same thing. "Yeah," I said. "It's possible."

It happened two hours later. At that point I had made little headway with Carla. Hearing Stinger and Cruz talking over the intercom as they returned from the alien ship, I decided to finish up and meet them in the airlock. They were already half out of their EV suits when I arrived.

"Any progress?" Cruz asked me through the open inner airlock.

"Not much," I answered glumly, wishing I had better news. Standing outside the cramped airlock, I watched as Cruz shrugged off the rest of his suit, plugged it into the bulkhead, and activated in the recharge cycle. "How about you? Find anything over there?"

"Nothing that's gonna help," Stringer answered. "We'll check the smaller ship next."

Stringer was only partway out of his suit. Cruz was giving him a hand when the inner airlock door slid shut. "Hey, Mac, that's not funny!" Cruz called through the observation port, slapping the hatch button on his side.

The door stayed shut.

I tried the button on my side. Same result. By now both Stringer and Cruz were staring through the glass. "I didn't close it," I yelled.

Stringer pressed his face to the window, attempting to check the outer control panel. "Try removing the—"

He never got to finish, because just then the EVAC alarm sounded.

"Get your suits back on," I shouted.

There was no hope for Cruz, and he knew it. In his last moments, as air was rapidly being pumped from the chamber, he tried to help Stringer back into his EV gear. They almost made it.

Unable to help, I watched in horror as their bodies suddenly swelled in the vacuum. Globules of frothy pink filled the airlock.

Hideous seconds passed, seeming like hours. And then it was over. The outer hatch swung open. Riding the last outrush of air, Stringer and Cruz drifted into the void.

I found Julie on the bridge. When I told her about Stringer and Cruz, she listened quietly. "How could that happen?" she asked when I was done, her voice trembling with shock.

"There's only one explanation."

"Carla."

I nodded.

"But for an accident like that to—"

"It wasn't an accident. The airlocks are under direct computer control. Carla, or whatever she's become, killed them."

Julie was silent for a long moment. "Can we shut her down?"

"Not completely, at least not without losing life support. But I'll lock her out of as much of the rest of the ship as possible."

"What can I do to help?"

I hesitated. I wanted to recover Stringer and Cruz before their bodies had drifted too far from the ship. But considering the situation, I was also reluctant to leave Julie alone. Still, I didn't see any other way. "I have to go EV to collect the bodies," I answered. "Monitor me from the bridge."

"Right." Then she asked something I had been trying not to think about. "What do we do if Carla shuts down our life support systems?"

"There's always cryo-suspension, at least till the research vessel arrives," I suggested. Like most Federation ships too small to have onboard medical facilities, the *Magellan* was equipped with a single cryo-suspension unit, a holdover from man's early ventures into space. Serving as an emergency backup, it could maintain an injured crew member in frozen stasis pending arrival at a medical base.

"There's only one unit onboard," Julie pointed out.

"I know. It won't come to that, but if it does, I want you to use it."

Julie shook her head. "We're in this together, Mac."

I could tell from the look in her eyes that there was no use arguing. Nonetheless, I made my way to the cryopod, set the controls on auto, and disconnected the computer-override cable—making sure Carla couldn't sabotage the pod if Julie needed to use it. Perhaps I was kidding myself, but I felt better after that.

The outer hatch was still open when I returned to the airlock. It took me twenty minutes to get the control panel disassembled and cut the computer leads. I didn't intend to end up like Stringer and Cruz.

Shortly after that I was suited up and floating in space outside the *Magellan*. Although I couldn't spot the bodies, I knew they had to be dead ahead. Julie was in contact with me over the radio. She informed me that she had two objects on the scanner around four kilometers out. I hit my thrusters and took off.

Once I had picked up some velocity, I shut off my jets and drifted in silence. Fifteen minutes later the bodies came into sight. Upon spotting them, I started my deceleration, winding up using more fuel than planned. I knew I would have to be careful on the return trip.

The bodies were tumbling, separated from each other by about twenty meters. I got a line on Cruz, then dragged him over and got a line on Stringer, too. I tried not to look at their faces.

With Cruz and Stringer in tow, I headed back, surprised at how distant the *Magellan* had become. At that distance the smaller of the alien derelicts was lost against the backdrop of space, but the huge warship was still clearly visible. The *Magellan* looked tiny and insignificant beside it. All at once something about the position of the ships struck me as wrong. At first I couldn't figure it out. Then I saw it.

The *Magellan* had moved. Her inertial-drive cylinder was glowing. "Julie, what's happening?" I shouted into my radio.

No response.

All the way back I kept trying to raise Julie on the radio, without success. Though tempted to increase my velocity, I knew if I didn't keep enough fuel in reserve to kill my speed once I arrived, I would overshoot the *Magellan* and wind up drifting forever in space. But if the *Magellan's* ion drive kicked in before I got back . . . well, I wouldn't get back.

Inexplicably, the *Magellan* never moved. The drive cylinder had shut down by the time I got back, but its thick metal rim still glowed a dull, angry red. After dragging Stringer and Cruz inside the airlock, I sealed the outer door and waited for the chamber to repressurize. As soon as air began seeping back in, I heard the piercing wail of the radiation alarm.

Leaving the bodies in the airlock, I rushed aft without removing my suit, wondering what could have caused a reactor leak. But deep down I *knew*.

Carla.

I found Julie on the deck outside the fusion chamber. She was horribly burned, but alive. Barely. I ripped off my helmet and gathered her into my arms.

"You . . . you made it back," she mumbled. Her face had escaped the terrible searing I saw elsewhere on her body, but dried blood caked her nose and mouth, and something was wrong with her eyes. "I . . . I can't see, Mac."

"You're going to be all right, Julie," I said, praying I was right. "What happened?"

Blindly, she reached up to touch my cheek. "Carla tried to move the ship. I cut the control cables, but she lowered the shields while I was in the reactor room. I got the shields back up, but . . ."

"You're going to be all right," I repeated softly. "Just hang on."

Cradling her in my arms, I carried her to the cryopod. "What are you doing?" she asked as I gently laid her inside.

"You're going to sleep. When you wake up, the research vessel will be here. Their med team will know what to do."

She struggled to sit. "Mac, before Carla attempted to move the ship, she shut down our life-support systems. You won't—"

"I'll get them back on," I lied, knowing I couldn't.

"There's only one pod. Don't waste it on me. I'm not going to make it."

"You're wrong, Julie. You're going to make it. And so am I."

I got the needle into a vein where her skin wasn't too badly burned and started the cryo-drip, then stayed with her while the clear fluid slowly emptied into her. We talked—me doing most of the talking, trying to maintain contact. Then we just sat, not talking at all.

When she was ready, I sealed the pod and initiated the stasis cycle. I watched as her eyes closed and her body relaxed and a film of frost formed on her skin. Then I left her. I knew what I had to do.

I tried not to rush, but I didn't have much time. Even working as quickly as possible, it took me several hours to move the *Magellan*. I'm not a pilot and without computer assistance it was mostly trial and error, but I eventually got the ship positioned exactly where I wanted.

The smaller of the alien vessels was larger than I'd first thought, turning out to be over two hundred meters in length. On closer inspection I saw how deeply its hull had been slashed. Through the open gashes I could make out some of the interior— a hellish block of gray-green crystal. Though I searched, nowhere could I see a means of entering.

I used mooring lines to lash the alien vessel to the opening of the *Magellan's* drive cylinder. It was slow work, but I got that done, too.

They say revenge is sweet, but I felt only bitterness and revulsion as I entered the computer bay and sat before the Omni. I knew it wasn't Carla anymore; it was something else, something alien. I could almost feel the hate radiating from whatever she had become. "I know you can hear me," I said. By then, with our life support systems inoperable, the ship's internal temperature had dropped to near freezing and the air was getting stale. "I know you're in there, and I want you to know what I'm going to do."

And then I told it.

Minutes later I fired up the *Magellan's* main inertial thruster, blasting the propulsive ions directly into the alien ship I'd lashed to our drive cylinder.

Before long, the alien vessel reestablished contact with the Omni. I could see the signal in the analyzer. I watched with satisfaction as it flickered and wavered and weakened as the alien ship began to glow a dull red in our thruster's exhaust. I hoped whatever was in that ancient ship was capable of sensing pain, of anticipating death. It even tried to communicate with me through the Omni at the end, calling me a carbon-based entity. I didn't bother to respond.

The ion engine ran for nearly an hour before the thruster cylinder overheated and shut down. I rechecked our position. With the *Magellan's* thrust being diverted by the alien vessel, we had only moved a few kilometers. But by then every circuit aboard the alien craft had been roasted, every memory bank incinerated, every electronic synapse destroyed.

Then I addressed the Omni one final time. "You're next."

I planned to turn it off, realizing that to do so would cause irreparable damage—not only to the computer, but to the *Magellan* itself. Nonetheless, I had to destroy every kernel of consciousness the alien had planted aboard our ship, whatever the cost. Grimly, I pried off the Omni's main panels and located the power cables. One by one, I severed them.

Does murder apply to terminating an artificial intelligence? I'm not certain, but after what had happened, I'd come to believe that in all ways that truly mattered, Carla was alive. She, and the presence we had discovered aboard the alien ship. So in a sense, what I did *was* murder—premeditated and deliberate.

But when the time came to do it, it was easy . . . and I would do it again.

* * *

I turned off the heater in my EV suit a while back. They say freezing is supposed to be an easy way to go. I guess I'll find out. And with any luck, maybe it won't be permanent. They revive people from cryo-suspension all the time, right?

At least there's a chance.

An icy numbness is creeping through my limbs, and a crust of ice has formed on the interior of my viewplate. If I peer through the bottom, I can just make out the *Magellan* floating at the end of my tether, her scorched captive close behind.

I acquired a slight rotation when I exited the airlock. I didn't bother to correct it. Within minutes the second alien vessel will rise again on my left, laden with her long-dead crew. I'm closing my eyes now. I don't want that ship to be the last thing I see.

The next time it comes around, I'll be gone.

*   *   *

SUBSPACE TRANSMISSION ST978.6.84

TO: COM CEN DIST 3, EARTH
FROM: FEDERATION RESEARCH VESSEL INTREPID, HORSEHEAD NEBULA D17.233.15

TEXT: FEDERATION SHIP MAGELLAN FOUND IN DERELICT CONDITION. CREW MEMBERS STRINGER AND CRUZ DEAD IN AIRLOCK. CREW MEMBER REAGAN ALIVE IN CRYO-SUSPENSION. WILL INTERROGATE REAGAN UPON CRYO-REVIVAL.

CREW MEMBER MCGUIRE'S FROZEN BODY RECOVERED FROM SPACE. CONCLUDE THAT MCGUIRE WAS RESPONSIBLE FOR DEATHS OF STRINGER AND CRUZ, INJURY TO REAGAN, AND SABOTAGE OF OMNI 4000 COMPUTER. WILL

NOT ATTEMPT TO RESUSITATE MCGUIRE AS NO PSYCHIATRIC FACILITIES AVAILABLE.

OMNI 4000 DAMAGE EXTENSIVE, BUT HAV EES#&* COMPLETED FULL DOWNLAOD OF ALL SALVAGEABLE FILES.

TWO ALIEN CRAFT FOUND AS REPORTED. EXPLORATION TO COMMENCE WQNNM UPON CORRECTION MKOPPP OF INTREPID AIRLICK MALFUNCTOINS.

END TRAMSNISSIOG.

Blue Skies

Rob pulled off the dirt road and wheeled his truck up a long gravel driveway, stopping in front of an old farmhouse. "Your turn, Matt," he said, glancing over at me.

"I did the last one," I protested, belatedly noticing his grin. As usual, Rob was jerking my chain. He knew I hated to do the asking.

Well, hate isn't exactly the right word. It made me . . . uncomfortable. For some reason whenever I asked a farmer's permission to hunt his fields, I felt I was intruding. The fact is, most farmers rarely refused us; usually they even told us where they'd last seen birds and whether the area had been recently hunted.

Rob cut the engine, set the brake, and swung out of the cab. "Guess it's up to me, then," he chuckled.

Sipping tepid coffee, I watched from the warmth of the truck as Rob crunched across the frozen driveway, mounted the porch steps, and knocked on the door. The farmhouse, a shabby, single-storied structure flanked by several ramshackle outbuildings—a barn, corral, and equipment shed—had a sad, lonely look to it. Like so many of the farms we visited, the newest thing about this one was a satellite dish sprouting like an inverted mushroom from under a roof eave.

The pickup lurched slightly as our dogs shifted in the back. Turning, I saw Max and Sammy staring over the tailgate at an ancient farm mongrel who had ambled out from behind the barn. Sammy rumbled deep in her throat. Max let loose a halfhearted bark.

"Quiet," I said, rapping on the glass so they knew I meant it. Both dogs lowered their ears and gave me their best "Who, me?" looks, then went back to conserving energy.

Not for the first time, I noticed how alike they seemed. Both were on the smallish side for Labrador retrievers, with broad black heads and intelligent golden eyes. Sammy was my dog; Max was a male pup from her one and only litter. Four seasons ago I had given eight-week-old Max to my hunting partner and best friend Rob, and then later had helped with Max's training. Max had turned out to be one of the finest bird dogs in the valley. Almost as good as Sammy.

Rob knocked on the farmhouse door again. Moments later a thin woman with a baby tucked in the crook of her arm opened the door and stepped out onto the porch. Rob started talking, gesturing toward the acreage behind the house. I couldn't hear what he was saying, but before long the woman was pointing into the fields too, her free arm sweeping an arc from the cut cornfields to a wide drainage ditch at the west end of the property. I smiled, deciding Rob should *always* do the asking. People simply liked him; that's all there was to it. From the looks of things on the porch, I suspected that by the time he was done talking, we would probably be invited for dinner.

By then the wind had picked up a bit, sending leaves skittering around the yard and raising billows of dust behind the barn. Hoping the weather didn't worsen as the day progressed, I glanced at my watch. Ten AM.

It had been calm when we had headed south earlier that morning, the sun barely cresting the mountains guarding the eastern flank of the Wood River Valley. We had stopped in Hailey for coffee and a couple of deep-fried apple fritters, then settled down for the drive. Over the seasons Rob and I had spent countless hours traveling to and from hunting spots, usually spending more time driving than hunting. Occasionally we rode in silence, but mostly we talked. Although you would think that after all those years we would have run out of things to say, we never did. They were enjoyable hours, time well spent.

Rob returned from the house, his eyes lit with excitement. "Good news, amigo. They just cut the corn, and nobody's hunted it since then. We've got those pheasants all to ourselves."

Pheasants are my favorite game bird—smart, challenging, and good eating. Getting the old butterflies-in-the-stomach feeling that for me invariably precedes a pheasant hunt, I gazed across the fields behind the house. Rob was right. The corn's having just been cut was a tremendous advantage. As long as corn is still standing on a big acreage like that, the birds usually stay well hidden, deep in the middle. The only way to flush them is to walk through the corn rows (if the farmer will let you), with other hunters waiting at the far end. Beaters and blockers. If you're a beater, it gets dicey when the birds start getting up. You can't see who's shooting on the other side of the cornstalks. All you can hope is that whoever it is, he waits until he sees blue sky before pulling the trigger.

Anyhow, now that the corn was cut, the birds had been forced to move to new cover in the irrigation ditches, fence lines, and brush bordering the field—areas two guys with good dogs could hunt effectively.

"How do you want to do this?" asked Rob.

I finished my coffee and thought a moment. "Normally I'd say we should hunt into the wind," I answered. "But something tells me there are birds in that ditch at the west end. Let's try that first."

Rob nodded. "Right. We can work the fences later."

We took a dirt access road to the northwest corner, parking a hundred yards from the main drainage ditch. By then the dogs knew the hunt was on. When I walked to the back of the truck for my gun and orange hunting vest, their eyes never left my face. I let the tension build a few moments. Then I grinned. "Let's go!"

I didn't have to tell them twice. Tails wagging, they leaped over the tailgate and hit the ground, wrestling with each other like pups—one on top, then the other. Thinking they looked more like twins than mother and son, I let them go at it awhile, venting some steam before the hunt.

"Ready, Matt?"

"Yep," I answered, shrugging on my vest and stuffing a handful of twelve-gauge shotgun shells into my pocket. "Soon as you get that rowdy dog of yours under control, we can do it."

Rob laughed. "It's that frisky bitch of yours causing all the trouble," he countered. "Let's go find some birds, Max."

At that, both dogs stopped playing. They knew it was time.

Rob cracked his over-and-under and shoved in two twenty-gauge shells. I headed toward the nearest drainage ditch, feeding ammo into my Browning automatic as I went.

"Aren't you forgetting something?" Rob asked.

"Oh. Right." I returned and closed my hand, meshed my knuckles with Rob's extended fist, then withdrew slightly and punched, fist to fist. It was a stupid ritual, but we had been doing it for years. Customary fist-bump completed, we set out. Soon we reached the weed-filled ditch, our dogs out front. Rob took one side; I took the other. Not expecting much to happen for a while, I wasn't paying attention. It cost me.

One of the first things you learn about hunting upland birds is to *always* be ready. Game birds, especially pheasants, can hide in the most measly cover imaginable, flushing when you least expect it. It's precisely this unpredictable element that makes pheasant hunting so much fun. Just when you think you have everything figured out, something unexpected happens. I had learned that lesson the hard way many times, so naturally when Sammy flushed a big rooster to my side of the ditch, I wasn't ready. I'd barely flipped off the safety and shouldered my gun when the bird disappeared behind a stand of Russian olive trees.

"Why didn't you shoot?" Rob called from the other side.

"Wasn't ready," I replied sheepishly.

"Damn," Rob muttered, giving me a disgusted look. I think Sammy gave me a similar look as well.

Not off to a good start, I thought. Nevertheless, we still had the whole farm to hunt, and now we knew for certain that there were birds around. We headed down the drainage ditch once more. It was a good-sized wash, dry now in the fall, narrow in spots and wide in others. Clumps of willows guarded its banks, with plenty of cover in between. Although at times I couldn't see Rob, I could hear him crashing through the undergrowth on the other side, and we managed to stay abreast. Sammy was down in the gully hunting in close, just as I'd taught her. It was a pleasure to watch her work.

We tramped along for a quarter hour without seeing any more birds. The air was crisp, but the sun had begun to warm things a bit, slanting through the cattails choking the gully and melting the frost on the exposed ground in between.

"Get ready, Matt," Rob warned as we approached a bend in the canal. "Max is on scent."

"Sammy is birdy, too," I called back, my pulse quickening. Sammy was definitely hot, her tail rotating in tight circles as her nose dragged her on an erratic path through the cover.

Walking quickly, I proceeded down the ditch. Before long I realized that the bird was running. It wasn't going to hold. We needed to push it hard or it would just keep running and never flush. I picked up my pace, stumbling after Sammy, trying to keep up. The end of the ditch was quickly approaching. Suddenly a thicket ahead exploded with a rush of wings. I had been poking my safety ever since Sammy had gone on scent, so this time I was ready.

Two birds came out on my side. I swung through the lead bird. A hen pheasant. I switched to the second. Another hen. Lowering my gun without shooting, I watched them sail off into the sage. An instant later I heard Rob fire once.

"Get one?" I called.

"Yeah. Must've led that sucker by ten feet. God, I'm good! Nothing came out on your side?"

"Hens."

"Well, the day is young," Rob called back, his tone saying I'd had my chance earlier and blown it.

In the excitement I had lost track of Sammy. When I didn't see her, I figured she had gone over to make Rob's retrieve. "Sammy over there?"

"Nope."

Sammy still had to be in the ditch. And if so, there was a reason. Taking off at a fast jog, I had covered half the distance to the bend in the canal when another rooster got up forty yards out, Sammy snapping at his tail feathers.

The bird turned downwind, his large size making his speed deceptive. I missed with my first shot, as usual not giving it enough lead. Knowing I would only get one more try, I doubled my lead on the bird, forced myself to keep the gun swinging, and pulled the trigger. This time I was right on target.

Flushed and out of breath, Rob joined me, smiling as he noticed Max racing out to beat Sammy to my rooster. The dogs wouldn't fight over a bird once it had been picked up, but until then both considered it fair game. Nonetheless, Max was faster, and I wanted Sammy to get the bird. I hit one long blast on my whistle. Both dogs stopped dead in their tracks, turned as one, and sat—eyeing me expectantly.

"Sam!" I yelled, releasing her. With that, Sammy took off at a full run and made the retrieve. Max stayed put. I swear Sammy flaunted that pheasant as she pranced past Max on the return trip.

"Poor Maxie," said Rob as Sammy sat beside me and delivered the bird to hand.

"Poor Max? I don't think so. He already retrieved *your* bird."

Rob blew one long, then two short blasts on his whistle, signaling Max to come in. "I know, but he wants to retrieve them *all.*"

"Tough," I laughed. "It's about time he showed his mother a little respect."

We set out once more, working a fence line downwind, then back to the northeast corner. Though we hunted the area thoroughly, we only scared up a couple more hens, possibly the ones we had seen earlier. After giving the dogs water, we tried the west edge of the cornfield, following an irrigation ditch bordering the stubble. A half hour later two roosters got up together—one to the left, one to the right—a perfect shooting situation. Rob fired first and dumped his into the fallow. The dogs immediately raced to retrieve it. I took my bird a split second later with a long going-away shot, but the rooster locked his wings and glided another sixty yards before falling dead in the cut corn rows.

Max and Sammy returned, Rob's bird in Max's mouth. Rob stuffed the pheasant into his vest pouch. "Get the other one?" he asked.

I nodded. "It's out in the stubble."

"Did Sam see it fall?"

"Nope."

"See if you can handle her to it."

"Okay," I replied. "It's been a while. She could use the practice."

I called Sammy to heel and lined her up on the fallen bird, my hand positioned just above her head to indicate the direction I wanted her to take. "Dead bird," I said. She stared ahead intently, focused and ready.

"Back!" I said.

Sammy took off like a shot. She ran straight for close to fifty yards before drifting to the right. I blew the whistle and stopped her. She turned and sat, waiting for directions. Using hand and whistle commands, I sent her left, then back again, straight to the downed pheasant. A field-trial champion couldn't have done better.

"Impressive," said Rob as Sammy returned with the rooster.

"You know it," I agreed. I had trained Sam, starting her at seven weeks, but in truth she deserved most of the credit. She had always been more than willing, wanting to please with all her heart. When she brought that bird back to heel, I thought I was going to burst with pride. As for Sammy—well, she simply delivered the pheasant to hand and started hunting anew. No big deal. As I shoved the rooster into my vest, I realized that of all the things I liked about hunting, I most enjoyed working the fields with my dog. Without her it wouldn't have been the same.

At that point Rob and I each needed one more bird to fill our limits, but over the past hour the wind had continued to rise. We were getting cold. We decided to speed things up by hunting the final irrigation ditch separately, beginning at opposite ends and working toward each other, pinching any runners between us. I don't normally like knowing someone's approaching with a gun pointed in my direction, but Rob and I had worked ditches that way before, and I trusted him. Plus it was an effective strategy.

Sammy and I hunted for the next twenty minutes without success. As I approached a right-angle bend in the ditch, I noticed Rob approaching from the left, still a few hundred yards out. Sammy was ahead of me, rounding the bend. I lost sight of her as she entered a thick clump of thistle. I took a shortcut across the stubble, planning to catch up with her on the other side.

I've mentally replayed what happened next at least a thousand times. It's always the same. For some reason I see it in slow motion: A bird gets up in front of Rob. It veers down the ditch, flying low. Rob's gun comes up. The bird falls. I hear Sammy yelp, then the shot.

I ran. I knew she was hurt. Even as a pup, she never cried. Never.

My heart was pounding when I reached her. By then she had crawled from the ditch and was lying on the ground licking her flank. I knelt beside her. She'd taken pellets in her hind leg, some in her side below her ribs, another near her shoulder.

Rob arrived moments later. "What happened?"

"Rob, you shot her."

"Jesus. I . . . I didn't see her."

"Why didn't you wait till you saw sky before shooting?"

Rob's face turned ashen. "I . . . I had to be at least seventy yards away. Those pellets couldn't have penetrated.

"I hope you're right," I said, examining Sammy's wounds. The worst bleeders were on her leg. They had already slowed considerably. Teasing back the fur, I checked her side. I found several round holes in her skin, wet red tissue glistening beneath. I couldn't tell whether the pellets had gone any deeper. Seventy yards was a long way. Maybe they *had* just bounced off.

Abruptly, Sammy rose to her feet.

"She's fine," said Rob, clearly relieved. "I told you she was okay."

"Let's go, girl," I said, praying Rob was right. I started walking, watching Sammy carefully. As usual, she took her position out front, glancing back to see which direction I wanted to take. She was moving well, not even limping.

"She's fine," Rob repeated.